For B,

I hope you love this one as much as my first!

Coming Home

a novel

Kay Tobler Liss

♡ Kay

Plain View Press, LLC
1101 W 34th Street, STE 404

www.plainviewpress.com
Austin, TX 78705

ISBN: 978-1-63210-106-8
ebook ISBN: 978-1-63210-102-0
Library of Congress Control Number: 2023944770

Cover photo by Kay Tobler Liss
Cover design by Pam Knight

To my brother, Toby, and
to my grandmother and mother
who continue to inspire me
in ways still being revealed

"The tree that moves some to tears of joy
is in the eyes of others only a green thing which stands in the way.
Some see nature as all ridicule and deformity,
and by these I shall not regulate my proportions,
and some scarce see nature at all.
But to the eyes of the man of imagination,
nature is imagination itself."

William Blake

The Meadow

Walking in the quiet woods, she comes upon a great meadow, the grass golden in the early autumn sun and nearly twice as tall as she. Smiling, she spreads her arms and leaps through the yielding shafts as they open a path for her. Suddenly out of breath, she looks around only to realize she doesn't know which way to go. She might even be lost, but doesn't feel frightened.

As she closes her eyes and tips her head to the sky, around she spins, arms like wings. She falls back, laughing, and gazes at the blue sky through the wild grass engulfing her. She imagines the meadow wrapping its arms around her now, feathery fingers brushing against her cheek.

In a voice that surprises her with its forceful, far-reaching clarity, she says, "I wish this moment never to end, for this is the happiest I'll ever be." Then, she hears the hard sound of a distant voice, calling her name. She doesn't want to answer, and hopes she'll never be found.

As Lydia looks out her brownstone window into the early morning light high above Columbus Avenue, she sees a dark bird suddenly fly by, ascend then disappear into the patch of steely sky above, somehow reminding her of the dream of last night, a dream she's dreamt before. Like many dreams, it began as a real place and event in her past, so long ago and far away that it's transformed into a fairy-tale lived only in the darkness and stillness of sleep.

Other than noting its familiarity, features, and general tone, she never gave this dream much thought before. Where was this meadow and how did it come to secure such a long-lasting foothold in the cave of her imagination? Why did she feel it was the happiest she'd ever be, lying in the meadow's light-filled midst, and then, in stark contrast, that she wanted to hide forever from the foreboding voice calling her?

Lydia glances at her watch. She'll have to rush to get ready for work now. Lately, she's always rushing to get ready.

Gulping down the last vestige of coffee in her cup, she unties her robe as she hurries to the bedroom. She used to take time to brush her long, reddish brown hair in a kind of ritual, just as she took time to think about what she was going to wear. There was a certain excitement she found in clothes, the way they looked on her, the way they made her feel. She even had developed a psycho-sensory system of colors and styles, choosing clothing to match what she sensed as the mood of the day. But somehow, that excitement had waned along with the idle, dreamy moments of morning. Whatever happened to be handy and respectably clean would do.

Today Lydia's lucky and has a seat to herself on the subway downtown. She opens her book of *The Collected Poems of Wallace Stevens*, a favorite to read on her way to work because of the solace she finds in the thought of him, in his 1950s' style drab gray suit and sensible dark tie, composing these enigmatic, fantastic lines of verse on his way to work in an insurance office.

. . . He rode over Connecticut
in a glass coach.
Once, a fear pierced him,
In that he mistook
The shadow of his equipage
For blackbirds. . . .
The river is moving.
The blackbird must be flying. . . .

Smiling, she looks past the gripping arms and stern faces through the smudgy window to the tunnel blackness streaming by. These words and images—elliptical, haiku-like, so light and airy yet dark and foreboding! Instinctively, her body begins to absorb and translate them: she imagines swift, circular leaps, arms arcing forward in unison with legs; the body becomes a river, undulating forward, then it's a lone bird, flying high in the sky, higher until it disappears finally from view.

She glances away from the gray computer screen to the big black clock on the wall. It's four-thirty. Two more paragraphs to edit.

"You're coming to the Christmas party, aren't you Lydia?" Ralph asks brightly, sticking his head into her cubicle.

"Oh, hi, Ralph. I forgot all about it. I don't know. I have to pack for a trip." She quickly turns her eyes away from him. He's so good-looking she can find herself staring without knowing she is.

"Come on, one quick toast. Where're you going, by the way?"

"To my grandmother's in North Carolina." God, what a nerd I must sound like, she thinks. He's probably going to Aspen or St. Barts.

"Great. Well, maybe I'll see you in a few."

3

Lydia doesn't like going to staff get-togethers anymore. It's not so much the people, though the younger ones, except for Ralph, are rather pretentious, unduly impressed with the idea of working for such a prestigious magazine as *Architectural Journal*; and the older ones lack the enthusiasm but have retained most of the pretentiousness, now hardened into a kind of impenetrability, as if they'd transformed into admirable architecture themselves.

No, it's not them as much as simply the work, which is what everyone, of course, talks about at the parties. It's all the puffery and superciliousness, inherent in writing about these fabulous homes and buildings inhabited by people with fabulous fortunes, that seep into the very flesh and blood of the writers. Yes, there was a kind of whirling, dazzling allure at first, like entering a Disney World or Land of Oz, but now this once glittering land appears more stultifying to her than a two-mile-long wheat field in Kansas.

"Here's a little something for you for Christmas, Harold," Lydia says to the tall, blue-uniformed doorman, handing him a gift. He's the one person in the building to whom she truly wants to wish a Merry Christmas, perhaps because he's the antithesis of her colleagues, so without pretense and refreshingly *real*, and because, after standing all day long opening the huge glass doors for the so self-important people, he displays the same amiable manner and erect dignity at five o'clock as he does at nine in the morning.

"Thank you, and a Merry Christmas to you, too, Miss Lydia." As if it were a precious gem, he holds the small golden package close to his furrowed face gleaming like a delighted child's.

She snaps shut the suitcase then gives the room a quick scan. The tennis racquet: usually there's at least one day warm enough to play. And to play with Daniel again—what fun that will be! Don't forget the bulging bag of Christmas presents, she thinks. Oh, and the one more gift to buy for Nans; she's the easiest to buy a gift for. The men are the hardest: every year after earnest pondering, Lydia inevitably resorts to the unimaginative box of Titleist or the latest book on improving one's golf swing. And Mom is nearly as difficult, maybe because she's so intractably self-denying—part of her martyrdom syndrome, Lydia believes—that she makes one feel almost guilty buying her anything. Nans always expresses pure glee at receiving a gift, raising her dramatically arched dark eyebrows and still-taut cheeks and exclaiming she's "tickled pink."

Suitcase and bag of presents in hand, Lydia walks the two blocks to Broadway and turns into a shop on the corner that sells crafts from Guatemala. She spots two enchanting metal sculpted reindeer, the ends of their antlers formed into little candelabras. Perfect for Nans, she thinks.

As she stands on the corner hailing a taxi for the airport, Lydia feels a drop of wet snow fall upon her cheek. Though it's rush hour in Manhattan, she can sense the air pregnant with that hushed stillness of impending snowfall. She turns her face upward and sticks out her tongue. Even if loaded with car fumes and whatever other poisons blanket this metropolis, the drop nevertheless tastes magical, and within its half-frozen form, the season's spirit begins to melt into her.

Along the Cape Fear

The plane descends beneath the clouds, the white lights of the runway beckoning in the blue-black darkness below, while off in the distance shine the night eyes of the sleepy southern city of Wilmington. Though it's been two years since she's been here, Lydia remembers the size of the city, judging from the span of its lights, to be about the same. She pictures the elegant, stylish face of this antebellum town, spared the ravages of the Civil War, but not entirely those of the twentieth century, a smoky industrial cluster hemming its outskirts.

As the plane banks south to land, a river, coursing through the heart of the city like a great artery from its mother sea, comes into view. Wending its way slowly northward is the incomprehensibly long row of lights that could only belong to an oil tanker bound for the city's deep port. The Cape Fear River, belying its name, looks incongruously tame through the tiny plane window. But surely, Lydia imagines, within its dark and winding banks lurk many a fearful tale.

Once over the bridge that crosses the river and out of the city limits, the road south from Wilmington is dark, dreary, and even scary at night. With no lights and very few houses along the way, Lydia finds she must be especially attentive at the wheel so as not to waver even a foot, lest she end up in the deep ravine paralleling the narrow road. Making visibility even worse, a thick fog wafts across the land from the river not far away.

The land between the cities in this part of North Carolina, with its forgotten cotton fields and lonely tin-roofed clapboard shacks, has a Gothic, eerie feel to it. Yet, still stronger than the air of eeriness is a kind of melancholy; perhaps, Lydia reflects, it arises from the vast disparity between the white-columned, pretty-mansioned cities and this defeated, tobacco brown land of brown inhabitants.

But, like gaudy phoenixes emerging out of the ashen darkness and above the rusty-roofed shacks, brightly lit billboards depicting an Edenic world of forever green fairways and happy golfers begin to loom along the roadside: Plantation Oaks, Your Dream Retirement Village; Relax and Live the Good Life at Southern Pines Plantation. The old cotton, tobacco, and rice plantations of a privileged white society reincarnated as modern meccas of well-off whites. She supposes she shouldn't be so cynical about the South, but when she travels through here, she can't help but think of leaders like Jesse Helms, the still active Ku Klux Klan and those four brave black men in a Greensboro, North Carolina diner where the civil rights movement began when she was ten years old.

How she wishes at times she had been old enough to take part in that movement. The anti-Vietnam marches, the women's and environmental movements of the 1970s meant a lot, but the civil rights movement loomed large in her mind. Now, in the late 1980s, the only cause that seems to hold meaning for most people she knows is to make a ton of money, then retire at forty to find inner peace in climbing mountains, keeping in shape, driving a nice car, and making even more money playing the stock market. But then, she thinks, at least they know what they want. That counts for something.

Suddenly the car veers off dangerously to the right, running along the edge of the ravine for a second or two. Not a good place to let your mind drift off, she reminds herself.

Finally, a sign for Southport. It's almost eleven o'clock. The town is all tucked in, the light on the wide, welcoming porch of nearly every house the only indication of life. As she remembers, everyone here, including her mother, grandmother, and great grandaunt, is in bed by nine-thirty.

She slows down to see if she might recognize the street where they live. Yes, Caswell Street. Giant live oaks laden with Spanish moss line the middle of the road and shine a lugubrious, silvery green in the faint moonlight. The houses, though mostly medium to large Victorians, seem small in relation to the trees. She approaches her grandmother's home, distinguished from the rest as it doesn't seem to be exactly Victorian or any identifiable style; it also has a larger front yard than other residences and an entrance facing the side rather than the street. Lydia smiles: how fitting Nans would live in a house with a distinct personality.

Not wanting to disturb them so late, Lydia had already arranged to stay the night at a motel. She also liked the idea of having a little time between arriving and seeing the family, a little time to prepare mentally, which is hard to do hundreds of miles away and in a place as remote from this life as New York City.

She turns back onto the main street and, a couple of blocks down where the road meets the river, she sees the lights of the Riverside Motel. She pulls into the small parking lot in front. The office door is open and a key with her name attached is on the desk.

It's a bright room, with white wicker furniture, a grass green rug and a wall of louvered windows looking out over the Cape Fear River. Lydia opens the door to the small porch where a green lounge chair quietly awaits its next occupant to sit back and surrender to the sight and sound of the river.

As she sinks into the chair, she gazes out across the water, which seems more like a wide sea here where the mouth of the river meets with Long Bay and the ocean is a little to the south. Faint rays from a lighthouse on distant Bald Head Island, the windblown land at the river's end, reach across to her through the fog. The air has that methane-rich smell common to the coastal South, that scent of all manner of secret life breeding and decomposing just below the surface.

How much this is like the people too, she thinks: her great grandaunt, grandmother, and mother who, belying their vibrant surface personalities, keep so many secrets tightly bound inside. Like the tiny creatures in the river's muddy banks, these secrets with time decompose, but never, never really die, and in fact, become part of the rich layer of matter that broadens and deepens over the years.

Some of this rich matter pushes new thoughts, new forms through to the life-giving air above, but most of it remains hidden below and forever unknown.

Gigi, Nans, and Great Grandaunt Virginia

Though the three had indeed turned their lights out by nine-thirty—and great grandaunt Virginia by eight-thirty—Eugenia lay in her bed staring into the darkness, as if looking for some small tasks she might have forgotten to attend to during the day.

In addition to the normal demands of tending to the house, her mother Zipporah and great aunt, she finally finished putting all the Christmas decorations in their proper places: the Santa Claus, his white beard sparse and red suit faded and frayed but eyes as bright blue after so many years, stationed in the chair he's occupied for untold Christmases; the pair of golden angels, with their flowing platinum hair and outstretched hands holding the candles that would be lit on Christmas Eve, reigned over the fireplace mantel; and the assorted bulbs and other ornaments were carefully positioned on the tree.

All the food for Christmas Eve dinner was peeled, cut, or stuffed and ready to be cooked. The linens on the beds for Lydia and Daniel were changed and bathrooms bedecked with the best towels in the house (though she felt a sting of shame that she simply couldn't match all the washcloths, hand cloths and bath towels). The linen tablecloth and napkins had been washed and pressed and the silver and brass polished. What else could be left to do?

Tracing the day's myriad comings and goings, of things touched and placed and duties performed, is finally making Eugenia's mind as weary as her body. As her eyelids begin to slip over her eyes, she has the same thought she has almost every night, though so dimly illumined in that foggy place between awake and asleep as to be never actually known, that what she had forgotten was no less than herself.

She's in a small boat, drifting down the river. A handsome man in a white linen suit and Panama hat is standing on the riverbank, waving to her, and saying cheerfully, "Goodbye Gigi, now don't be afraid, and don't you forget you'll always be my best girl." She waves back, trying to be brave, fighting back the tears. She drifts around a bend, the man no longer in sight. She finds a piece of paper and some watercolors in the boat and begins to paint the trees along the river, the wildflowers, and birds, even a crocodile whose eyes she sees peering above the water in the distance. She smiles now, even laughs, as she ponders the curious crocodile she's created.

Eugenia awakens, eyes wide with the look of having seen something utterly fantastic. But her thoughts now race to what is real and the idea that she'd forgotten something becomes quite alarming. After all, it is Christmas Eve day, and Lydia and Daniel will be arriving soon. However, she's reminded of something else, the outline of which is vague but the feeling strong: of a child's seemingly unabatable sadness followed by sudden lightness, laughter, and the flight of birds. Lacking more substance, the feeling drifts away swiftly as her thoughts turn back to the imminent arrival of her children: Daniel brings a smile to her face while Lydia, well, it's always more complicated, a wanting to smile but then something getting in the way—she doesn't know what and now it's probably too late to ever know.

The light's just beginning to filter through the gauzy, once white but now graying curtains as she quickly throws off the sheets to confront another day.

What time is it? What the devil difference does it make anyway? Zipporah laughs to herself in the faint light. You'd think at this advanced age I'd finally not give a damn about what time it is. Realize I'd even achieved some measure of freedom, released from living within the confines of seconds, minutes, hours, even a reasonable number of years. But instead, more a *prisoner* of time do I become.

She gazes at her knotty fingers, slowly opening and closing them, then around the bedroom crowded with pictures and furniture she's faithfully carried over so many roads and years and squirreled into this final lair.

A game she plays over and over, she says to keep her memory from going to complete mush, is to trace the path of each item from its time of origin to the present. But all the details of each stop along the way must be completely recreated too: the room it was in, the place it had in that room, etc. Or in the case of a photo, the time, place, circumstances, whatever she could summon up. Occasionally, even new things she had never recalled before would come to her, at once exciting and unsettling her and causing her to wonder: How can my past be filled with so many things I still don't know?

She hears her daughter stirring in the kitchen, putting the kettle on for tea. It's a good, familiar sound, yet, despite this— not to mention her much-lauded stoicism—it almost brings a tear to her eye.

"Dear Lord, could this be the day?" Virginia asks out loud as she stares up at the high ceiling through her blurry eyes that blink slowly, straining as if to decipher a cryptic message written there.

"Now, what possibly could be your purpose in having me lie here like this, half blind and decrepit and all knotted up? I hope it's not just a severely warped sense of humor. Hah," she laughs at this bit of existential comedy. "Wouldn't that be the kicker to beat all? But, if I think it's even more droll than you—and, in case you didn't know, a droll sense of humor is what I'm most noted for in these parts—then tell me, who's goin' have the last laugh?"

Still Shots

The loud honk of the foghorn from Bald Head Island and an incipient cool dampness in the air rouses Lydia from a deep sleep. As she opens her eyes to the view across the river, she's momentarily disoriented, but then smiles at the thought she had been so relaxed that she fell asleep in the lounge chair *au plein air*. Of all the fond associations she kept of Southport, the opportunity to relax so completely was the most salient. This was all the more remarkable to her because if her stay extended beyond a few days, the time spent in the company of her mother, rather than relaxing, became more vexing. Yet somehow, the sultry air, the fullness of the idle quiet and stop-action sort of pace—as if the town existed in a long-past time and space—seemed to nullify any countervailing effects.

It's too early for The Ship's Chandler, the restaurant attached to the motel, to be open, so after showering and changing clothes, Lydia decides to walk down Main Street to see if she can find a place for coffee, though she doesn't expect to on Christmas Eve day. The fog billowing off the river up the street shrouds the gray, weather-worn buildings in another layer of gray. Suddenly, a pink and violet painted storefront pops out of the mist. Java Juncture, the vibrantly colored letters say, along with a small sign saying Open. Behind a pink marble counter with two large coffee urns and baskets of puffy croissants is a young man with shoulder-length hair.

"I'm so glad to see a real coffee shop in town."

"We moved down from Raleigh last year. It was getting too big-city-like," the young man says.

"Well, this is probably the one feature of a big city I'm glad to see here. I'd like a cappuccino and a croissant, please."

"Even in the last year, two new restaurants opened up in town, a Thai and a Tuscan. Both are excellent."

"I hope that doesn't portend hordes of upscale urbanites wanting to find peace and quiet in the country. I'd hate to see Southport change."

"Well, a little change isn't bad. If you lived here, you'd probably agree." He hands her the coffee and croissant.

Lydia looks at him thoughtfully. "You know, you're absolutely right. Mine is a completely selfish view. I like coming here because it's a trip into the past, where time seems to have stood still. Coming from a big city, especially like New York, change is happening every moment. It can be energizing but draining as well."

Sitting at a table, she gazes through the window to the street, the fog rising above the buildings now allowing a clearer view. Perhaps, she thinks, it's even deeper than that. Yes, it's also about wanting to stop the action because maybe, just maybe, there's some picture way back in the past that, if one could hold it perfectly still for a moment, it might be that final puzzle piece to make the scattered, inchoate story of a life make sense.

With his eyes fixed firmly ahead as he drives down the highway in the early morning light, Daniel observes there's a point in his peripheral vision where it becomes profoundly difficult to tell whether he's passing the world by or the other way around. It's one of those rare, eerily still moments when he suddenly sees himself from outside rather than inside his own head, disorienting him enough to feel pushed to a kind of metaphysical edge. Perhaps, he thinks reassuringly, the apparent confusion has more to do with the scene itself: the hypnotic effect of the endless dark forest of elongated, spooky-looking southern pines streaming by.

He turns his thoughts to Christmas. How great it's going to be to see Lydia; though they argued about most everything, it had been two years since they'd seen each other, and besides, the arguments were never serious enough to make them any less fond of each other. When they were growing up together, it seemed to, but not since, yes, since Evan died.

Enough thinking about that. Back to Christmas. Christmas is such a great time. Being a traditional kind of guy, Daniel loves Christmas, gets excited about it almost like a kid—the tree, the presents—though it certainly isn't the same in the South as it was growing up in the North. Sleigh bells and reindeer don't seem appropriate in Savannah, Georgia where he lives, but at least Southport is a little farther north.

Then—perhaps it's the darkness of the forest whirring by— he's stunned with the sadness of how different this Christmas will be: Cole is spending it with his mother this year.

He picks out a CD randomly from the glove compartment and pops it into the player. Miles Davis's "Kind of Blue." A corner of his mouth turns up as he speeds on down the road.

Greetings

About to knock on the door, Lydia notices the now rusty old sleigh bells—at least her mother always said they were sleigh bells—hanging from the door, just as they had been hung every Christmas on the front door of the house where Lydia and her brothers grew up. Under the warm sunny skies of the South, surrounded by a lush green lawn and lots of leafy trees and shrubs, how odd the bells appear, she thought. Yet, at the same time, they seem quaint and comforting in their evocation of The Happy Family of long ago. But isn't there something very odd, she thinks, about mother perpetuating this homey image?

There it is again. Every time she's about to see her mother, the pleasure is pre-empted by an edge of cynicism, a slight bitterness grown stale with age that she'd honestly prefer not to taste any longer. But it lingers on, stubbornly clinging to its own sort of tradition.

She knocks on the door.

"Hello, darling. How wonderful to see you!" Gigi greets Lydia in her exuberant, warm southern manner. How much more "real" this manner seems to Lydia here than it had seemed in the cool northeast where Lydia felt her mother learned to suppress it somewhat. There was something else, too, that made her mother appear more "herself" here than in the North, a sad secret, Lydia recalls, her mother hadn't articulated in twenty years of marriage and finally confessed one day to her daughter: she had always felt a sense of intellectual inadequacy in the company of her husband and his sophisticated northeastern friends. Such spontaneous sympathy Lydia had felt for her mother in that moment!

"Merry Christmas, Mom." She hugs her. It's always a bit of a shock at first to see her mother—the graying hair, a certain dullness and some wrinkling in her once luminescent face. The change seemed so dramatic, from a woman of such fairytale-like beauty—a brunette, brown-eyed, Marilyn Monroe, as she was often described—to this aging woman of sixty-seven. But there is a beauty that remains, in the empathetic eyes, the generous smile—yes, especially in the smile, Lydia thinks.

As they walk inside, the faded Santa with the still bright blue eyes and crimson cheeks greets Lydia from his wingback chair. She remembers that as a contemplative, though most adults thought melancholy, child she would stare at his unnaturally jolly face and wonder about the nature of happiness: What if humans spent more of their lives giving gifts—would they be happy too?

"The house looks wonderful, Mom. I should have tried to get here earlier to help you." Although she truly meant the latter, Lydia realizes she said it also out of another habit of mind, an age-old dynamic that sucks her and her mother into its mutually compelling forces: Lydia, always the selfish, willful child, so wrapped up in her own little world that she rarely considered those around her (most of all, of course, her mother), responds to assuage some unassuageable guilt; and by so doing, allows Mother the opportunity to indulge in her by-now quite perfected self-denial.

"Oh, well, I am rather tired." Gigi brushes the back of

her hand against her forehead and breathes deeply, a gesture faintly theatrical, reminiscent of those elegant screen heroines of the past.

"You know, Mother doesn't get out of bed much anymore, and of course Aunt Virginia can't do much either, so it does leave me with quite a bit to do. But," she smiles now wanly, "I don't really mind. After all, somebody's got to do it, and we can't afford for someone to come in, just a nurse for a couple of hours a week to help in bathing Gina."

"As we've said before, Mom, Daniel and I would be glad to chip in for more help. Perhaps it's time to send Aunt Virginia to a nursing home."

"Oh no, she wouldn't stand for it, and besides, the cost is so prohibitive. I wouldn't want to burden you two with such an expense."

Lydia knows it's useless to argue about this, no matter how logical her argument, because this isn't so much about logic or money or anything pragmatic, but about her mother's need to feel she is serving a purpose, even if it means denying herself.

"Come, let's go see your grandmother and great aunt. They've been so excited about seeing you and Dan, they could hardly contain themselves all week, which naturally meant they had even more instructions than usual for me." Gigi laughs, trying to sound lighthearted.

Propped up against the pillows, Zipporah's face, in spite of its paler tone, looks to Lydia not that much older than two years before, and still so startlingly beautiful. Perhaps it has something to do with the fact Nans is thin and angular featured, more like a Greta Garbo to her daughter's Marilyn Monroe, and that she is of a generation that didn't expose their bodies to the skin-aging sun. But the answer, Lydia suspects, has less to do with body and more to do with mind and spirit.

Yet there is something, she suddenly realizes, very different about her grandmother. Yes, the incredible auburn hair, so thick and waist-long, that Lydia loved to brush as a girl when her grandmother unwound the crown of braids upon her head, is now cut shoulder-length and gone almost completely gray. How much frailer, less self-assured Nans appears now, as if her Herculean hair had contained a secret to her power.

"Hello, sweet potatoes. Don't look so scared to see me, now. I know I look like a witch, but that's nothin' new. Come give me a kiss." Nans could always make you smile, take any fear away. Lydia leans over to kiss her on the cheek: the skin so fine, the bones pushing up farther with time.

"I certainly enjoy getting your fancy magazine. What I really like, to tell you the truth, is imagining how I would redecorate the rooms in the pictures. Pretty uppity of me, isn't it?" She giggles. "But it keeps the rusting old mind going and sort of brings me back to being at the museum and arranging all that miniature furniture in the dioramas," she says, now gazing off at an elaborately carved rocker in a corner of the room, as if it were a dear friend.

"I remember how privileged I felt when you let me help you at the museum, Nans. You know, I never put it together before, why I ended up working for an architectural magazine. But that is probably why. Amazing! Well, I'm glad I finally figured out the reason for at least one choice in my life." She notices out of the corner of her eye that her mother, unable to find any humor or lightness in this confession, has raised her eyebrows in a look of mock surprise.

One never to miss the emotional nuances in the expressions and comments of those around her, Zipporah's face twitches slightly. She seems to Lydia to be even more finely tuned now, as if the passing of time and her thinning skin have made her more sensitive. And, perhaps for this reason, her grandmother's response to these moments has always been to grab some strand of self-deprecating humor with which to escape, staying mainly down the middle.

"Sweet potatoes, I could live a hundred more years and probably still not know the reasons for goin' down most of the roads I went down." She stares off dreamily now at the chair in the corner. "Maybe that's why I ended up working at the museum, because it gave me a way to *arrange* things, particularly at that time in my life when...."

She stops suddenly, as if realizing she's stepping too far into the realm of the confessionally philosophical. She turns toward Lydia, her expression changing into one of childlike glee, and claps her hands once.

"Now, tell me all about my old stompin' grounds New York City. Is it still the most exciting place in the world to be?"

Captivated by what her grandmother was about to say, Lydia is disoriented by this sudden change of subject. How frustrating it is, being lured into learning some fascinating and profound bit of Nana's past, only to be abruptly cut off in mid-stream, she thinks. And as the directly posed personal question is frowned upon, Lydia has to hope for the occasional oblique crosses into that too-confessional realm that allow some light to fill in the dark patches of her familial past.

Reorienting herself, she responds, "Yes, probably, in terms of human energy—to work, to compete, to create. But somehow, none of it is very exciting to me anymore. I don't really do anything except go to work, and that's not very exciting anymore either. I've actually begun to feel quite guilty about it, like someone with an abundance of food on her plate, most of which goes to waste." Lydia can feel her mother's disapproving eyes upon her, and her grandmother is giving her a puzzled look: Lydia's stepped over that time-honored line, into the too serious and personal.

"Well, now you better go see Aunt Gina before she makes

a fuss. She's gettin' awfully touchy about people rememberin' her, though I guess I'm no one to talk." Nans scrunches up her face into a mischievous smile.

"Funny how us oldies get. You'd think, forgettin' as much as we do, we'd understand people forgettin' us. But we...now go on, sweet potatoes. Go see Gina."

As Lydia approaches her great grandaunt's room, she hears someone talking in the high-pitched, bell-like voice of a child and with all the tone and emphasis of conversing. "Harry, now I hope you're lookin' after Gordon. He needs lookin' after, even if he is a full-grown man. You better, or else I'll be after *you* soon. You hear me now, sugar?"

Lydia knocks as she peeks in the door hesitantly. "Aunt Gina?"

"Come on in. Is that you Lydia? Forgive me, darlin'. I know I must sound plum crazy, talking to Harry and Gordon, long since gone from this world, but I figure I better give them fair warning I'm coming soon." She blinks her lash-less eyes a few times, not so much to try to see better outwardly, but rather to clarify some inward reality.

"You know, it's taken me nearly a century, but to tell you the truth, I don't really give a gosh darn if people think I'm a little nutty. Mighty good feelin' to be free of that, let me tell you, sugar. Hah!"

Gina's laugh has the rough, sardonic sound of a crow's caw. She sees Lydia only impressionistically through her blurred vision. Strange, Gina thinks, how the world beyond this one I see only in my mind would appear more in focus, even more palpable, than this one right in front of me.

Raising her claw-like hand, slowly moving the long, yellow-nailed fingers as if feeling for some incorporeal entity in the air, she ponders the even larger paradox: that the more days spent on this earth, one would reasonably expect the more familiar the world would become, yet in truth, the stranger and stranger it becomes.

Lydia meets her hand in mid-air and holds it for a moment.

"Did your brother tell you when he'd be arriving?" Gigi asks, her voice ascending in a note of feigned cheeriness amid her nervous clanging of pots and ringing of silverware in the kitchen.

"No, I last talked to him over a month ago. But don't worry. He'll be here soon, I'm sure," Lydia reassures her, knowing nothing will until he arrives.

Lydia looks away and down at the worn, brownish linoleum floor, though deeply scuffed and torn around the edges, its pattern still easily discernible. She's surprised she still feels this double-edged pain: for Daniel having to endure her mother's obsessiveness, but more for herself never having to. She tries to dismiss it—it makes her feel so pathetically childish: the neglected little girl hungering for attention, the jealous sibling. God, she thinks to herself, I mean I'm thirty-eight years old! Get over it!

But this clinging vine has grown thick and resilient with time.

Above the kitchen noise, a ringing sound is heard. Everyone is quiet for a moment. Then Zipporah claps her hands and Gigi says, "That must be Daniel at the front door, at last!"

Lydia murmurs, so that no one can hear, "You'd think it was God, or at least Santa Claus!"

The Missing

"Daniel, would you say the blessing?"

"Maybe Nans or Aunt Gina would like to, Mom. I think it's only proper to defer to the older and the wiser," he says with a nod to them.

"No, darlin', in these parts it's proper to defer to the man at the head of the table, and since you're the only man here, you're it," Gina responds in her child's voice from her wheelchair where she's propped up with pillows, her arms barely reaching the level of the table.

"Well, some customs are just too good to ever die." Daniel looks mischievously at Lydia. His broad smile and the way he squinted, his honey-colored eyes seeming to smile too, reminded her of Evan in that moment.

"I know you actually mean that, Dan. It's a good thing you live in the land of southern belles, my charming brother, because you wouldn't make it to first base with the women up north," Lydia retorts lightheartedly, though her mother glares at her with her precious-Daniel-protector glare.

"Thank you, Lord, for this Christmas dinner, and for all of us gathered together here, and to those loved ones who aren't, our thoughts are with them. Amen"

Everyone begins to eat quietly, not wanting to mention the most obvious one missing, and the one his doting maternal relatives had keenly anticipated coming: Cole, Daniel's nine-year-old boy. The one Lydia most misses is her father. Gigi was gracious enough to invite him, but as usual, he declined.

As she gazes at the brightly flickering red candle before her, Lydia notices that, though the flame seems to dance wildly at random, after a while a pattern can be perceived, an elliptical returning to a central point. With the passing of so many years, she thinks, it should get easier, this having to choose with whom to spend holidays. But it never does, always looping back through time to its point of origin. When Dad is the one not chosen, she finds it especially hard—after all, he's the one who's all alone, though he insists he doesn't mind, at least at Christmastime: Christmas has always been a mixed occasion emotionally, he says, ever since his sister died on Christmas Eve when he was twenty-six.

She thinks about all those years he tiptoed down the staircase in the middle of the night to place gifts under the tree, then smiled upon his children as they gleefully opened them, all the while his attention only partly present. She pictures him sitting strangely aloof, outside the circle, a subtle cloud of sadness about him at this quintessential moment of family togetherness and festiveness. And now, the trail of sadness has only lengthened, with his wives all since having taken their leave and even one of his children, Evan, having left this world entirely.

Evan: Lydia is certain her mother and maybe Daniel also miss him at this very moment. Once, in a rare confessional and intimate moment with her daughter, Eugenia admitted she communes often with Evan's spirit, though "spirit" did not seem quite the right word: it was something more palpable, something closer to *him*.

The silence becoming a bit too eerie for him, Daniel asks Lydia, "Would you please pass the cranberry sauce? So, how's life in the big nasty city?"

Why is it, she thinks, that no one in my family—except perhaps Aunt Virginia—is able to put a name to the missing, a name to what's hidden in their emotional crypts? Isn't it like being partly dead, this part of us kept away from the air, denied the breath of life utterance would give? And is it fair to those we keep buried in these crypts? Maybe instead of answering Daniel's question I should ask him how Cole is or say I miss Evan, his smile that lit up all in its path.

Lydia feels the fire of these thoughts flickering intensely like the candleflame before her. But then, the so familiar airiness of an anticlimactic denouement she experienced in the company of family members, settles inside her.

Resigning herself, she asks playfully, "Why do you insist on describing New York as nasty, Dan? To tell you the truth, I'm not the right one to defend it either. In fact, I'm pretty tired of it. But then where does one go? Let's say I wanted to live in a town like Southport. What could I do?"

"Why, you could go shrimpin' or crabbin', though they say the crabbin' isn't so hot anymore," Virginia says with a wry smile. "All kiddin' aside, with your talents, the only thing you could probably do is work for the little weekly *The Cape Fear Gazette*. If you didn't mind traveling, you could commute to Wilmington and work on the daily newspaper there."

"She's only working for one of the most prestigious magazines in the world," Zipporah pipes in. "There're probably swarms of people love to have her job, isn't that right, Lydia? Seems to me, what's more important is what you're doing, not where you are, sugar."

The simple clarity of this last thought stuns Lydia. She stares into the candleflame, its seemingly chaotic movement now revealing a hidden order. Suddenly the image of dancing in a meadow amidst tall golden grass waving in the wind comes to her.

"Perhaps, yes. But can't one have both the what and the where?" Lydia asks dreamily.

"You could probably do what you're doing from anywhere, Lydia. Set up a home office, e-mail your edited articles. I would actually do better in New York, closer to Wall Street. But I do okay in Savannah with the small investment firm I'm in, and I like it there, besides the fact...well, of course, Cole's mother likes it there too." Daniel takes a big sip of his wine.

"Anyway," he continues, "I couldn't take all the dirt and crime in New York. And the rude people. Down here, everyone is so polite and hospitable."

"Now, that's sure the truth, sugar," Gina says, lifting her wine glass shakily. "I'll drink to that."

"Just a second there, Gina. Now, I may be a southerner born and bred, but that's just not so. You've never lived in New York City, nor have you Daniel, so neither of you really know what you're talking about," Zipporah dissents in her good-humored but slightly scolding manner. "I lived there for twenty years, and people in the neighborhood were as friendly as anyone here. And if they didn't like you, they'd let you know, not like here where they'll put on a smiling, polite face even though they don't actually like you 'cause you're different than them. This is why, besides the fact that a fair amount of white people down here secretly wish we were back in the good old plantation days, black people aren't ever goin' be treated as equals here."

As she often is by her mother's bold pronouncements, Gigi looks visibly embarrassed, biting her bottom lip, while Gina is clearly amused, shaking her head and smiling. Daniel, however, is indignant.

"But the thing is, black people are the ones who don't treat us as equals now. I feel like we're the ones being discriminated against. When I walk down the street in Savannah, I sense it, even when I try sometimes to smile at them, show some friendliness."

"Maybe we deserve it, getting a taste of our own medicine," Lydia rejoins. "It might be good for our humility."

"I think you got that right, Lydia, yep. A good thing to learn, humility, and the one thing we humans seem unable to learn enough of," Zipporah says.

"How could it be that good if it's so close to the word humiliate?" Daniel asks jauntily, thinking he's gotten one up on them.

Not usually one to lack a response, Zipporah looks puzzled, her mouth bunching to one side and forehead furrowing. She peers out of the corner of her eye toward Lydia, the word expert in the family, for some help.

"Since the root of the word, humus, is Latin for earth, then one can say that any word with this root must mean a returning to the earth in some way, a remembering of what is at the base and the beginning of everything, therefore to what is common ground. It's really a beautiful idea, you know, when analyzed like that: humble, humility—why, even the word human. That by remembering where we all came from, we might find understanding, compassion. That maybe the earth, ultimately, is our best teacher."

All gaze at her with expressions of hazy befuddlement, except for Zipporah who brings her palms together in a soft clap. They turn toward their plates and quietly continue eating.

Lydia recalls the image of dancing in the meadow again and sees with searing clarity that she, and perhaps everyone at the table, though present, are also missing—from themselves.

Sounds

Lying in her bed looking out the half-windows of her attic room, unable to fall asleep along with the rest of the now slumbering household, Lydia listens for the sound of the Cape Fear River. The haunted, lonely clang of a channel buoy in the current calls out across the waterway, as if for something in that mute and murky world to answer it. The sound seems to mimic, eerily, one she can hear inside her: a plaintive cry for something past, drifted into a forgotten sea; or is it more like something yearned for in the fog-filled distant future? Perhaps it's from neither past nor future but from somewhere in-between, the buoy's elegiac tone alluding to something precious mistakenly believed to have been missing from her past but, in truth, was still there, waiting to be realized.

She closes her eyes, hoping the sound would take shape in her mind, bring her in touch with whatever was trying to emerge from the deep.

But try as she might, the musty attic air, some fabulous beaded and feathered gowns of great grandmother Ceci hanging along a rafter, as if waiting to be embodied in a second life, and once-lustrous mahogany furniture buried beneath dust in a corner, all conspire to enclose her in their memory.

Besides, attics feel familiar to her because they were where she often ended up in family abodes: the attic in the first family house where she had stayed when visiting, after her father had remarried and the new daughter had taken over Lydia's room; then, in the big Victorian house her mother had moved to after the divorce, Lydia had a bright, airy room, but upon returning from boarding school one Christmas vacation, she found it had been rented, again relegating her to the only room not taken—the attic. She actually grew to like that attic, mostly because of the skylight above her bed through which she watched and felt encouraged by the stars and moon.

As she looks through the half-window at the outline of darkened trees and the veil of night sky, a thought occurs to her: maybe living in attics has contributed to feeling much of my life separate and apart from others, which has surely contained its loneliness; but then hasn't it also offered me a vantage point to see above and beyond what others might see?

A closer sound, a kind of low groan, suddenly intrudes upon Lydia's senses. It's from Zipporah's room. She jumps out of bed and hurries down the steep stairs. Slowly opening her grandmother's door, she finds her curled up in the bed on her side.

Lydia sits on the edge of the bed and gently touches her shoulder. "Nans, what's wrong?"

Zipporah flinches and opens her eyes widely. "Lydia? Oh, I'm so sorry I woke you up. Well, it's not anything new, but it is getting worse. I'm far enough away from Aunt Gina's and Eugenia's rooms that they don't hear me. I don't want them to know 'cause I don't want them fussin' and worryin' over me, or else sendin' me to some godforsaken nursing home."

"That's the last thing Mom would do, Nans. She'll take care of you and Aunt Gina to the very end. You know, it's that stubborn, self-sacrificing bent the women in our family seem to have, at least until I came along."

"Oh, don't be so hard on yourself, Lydia. You probably have it too, sweet potatoes."

"Believe me, Nans," she laughs lightly, "it's one family trait I'm glad I *don't* have."

"Funny how the men have always been just the opposite, always doing as they darn well pleased." Zipporah pauses. "To be fair, though, I guess I had my share of doing what I darn well pleased." She sighs and then winces in pain.

"So, the truth is, Lydia, I've got an aneurism in my stomach. I take some pain killers, but there's nothing else I can do 'cause I'm just too old to have an operation. It will eventually rupture, and I think soon. I've been tellin' your mother I just have bad ulcers when I get pain during the day. But I mostly get them at night, thank the Lord. My time is comin' any day now, I know. Hah, I was hoping to outlast Gina, but she always had the better constitution. Maybe it's more 'cause she didn't indulge in the bourbon and the cigarettes like I did.

"Anyway, listen, sweet potatoes: I need your help. I'd like to get your dad and Ben here—remember him, the little boy I used to take care of and Daniel's best friend when they were growing up? The sooner they come, the better, but I don't want Eugenia and Gina knowing why. Gina would probably be okay, but you know your mother—she'd be hysterical. There are cousins and a nephew out in Michigan, whom I love dearly, but they can come later to the funeral. So, what do you think, can you manage it?"

Lydia encloses her grandmother's hands in hers: boney, slightly quivering, Zipporah's hands feel cold to Lydia, except for the fingertips; the once hot fire of life that coursed through her body now no more than a burning ember at its ends.

It seems at once an awesome privilege and burden to Lydia, to be the one chosen for this secret knowledge. A conspiracy of death. A shiver runs through her. She looks into her grandmother's clear, penetrating, modestly imploring eyes that appear to say after ninety-one years of being so much at the mercy of this and that happening, I can at last have control over this one, final act.

Lydia places her free hand on top of her grandmother's, squeezing it slightly.

.

Calling the Missing

"Oh, it's just lovely, Lydia. But you really needn't have gotten me anything, you know," Gigi says as she holds the bright red sweater across her chest.

"Yes, I know, Mom, but I wanted to, and I remembered that you always looked so great in red."

"Ah, maybe once. But I don't look great in anything anymore, but who cares, right?" she laughs a little unsurely.

"Absolutely got that right, Gigi. Too bad we only seem to learn that lesson when we're old and considered kinda' bonkers anyway," Gina says. For such a tiny, bird-like creature, she lets out a surprisingly man-size guffaw.

"Oh, speak for yourself, Gina. Just 'cause you're nuttier than that Christmas fruit cake over yonder, don't put me in the same mix," Zipporah responds. They both laugh heartily. Lydia glances at her grandmother, thinking that, though this teasing banter wasn't at all out of character, it betrayed a slightly manic tone.

"Thanks for the golf book, Lydia," Daniel says with slightly forced enthusiasm. "A little inspiration, just what I need. I'm not sure about *The Inner Game of Golf* though. It always seemed to me, you work on your mechanics—your swing and shoulder turn, your grip and stance, the outer things—and then your game gets better."

Even as he so confidently utters these words, a faint voice inside him whispers that there really is something more, more than just the "outer things."

"It seems to me, as in everything, the mechanics are only half the game, Dan," Lydia says. Noticing her mother begin to give her the predictable Daniel-protector gaze, despite the fact Lydia had tried hard not to sound in the least judgmental or condescending, she quickly offers a self-deprecatory example.

"Take tennis, for instance. I know how I can lose a game when I'm either too anxious to win, getting down on myself too much, or else too relaxed, not focused or caring enough about playing well. I think with golf the mental game might be even more refined, for there's less room for error in a swing. Anyway, speaking of tennis, I hope you brought your racquet, Dan. I've been playing indoors to keep my game tuned. Maybe I could give you, my tennis guru, a run for your money." Gigi smiles at this.

"I haven't been playing at all," Daniel says somewhat distractedly. He's thinking about this inner dimension idea, how it feels like a foreign land, but one from which vague signals are being sent—he flashes back to that weird moment driving down the highway past the spooky southern pines.

Gathering himself, he says, "I thought tennis was interfering with my golf game—the different muscles one uses, etcetera. But I would have played a few games with you, Lydia, if I'd thought to bring my racquet."

"Mom always keeps some old racquets around, don't you?"

"Well, yes. They're old, but maybe a couple of usable ones."

"We'll figure it out. Maybe we'll trade off using my racquet, to make it fairer. I could use some exercise after that great dinner last night. How about we make our Christmas calls then hit the courts?"

"Sure. I guess I'll call Cole now," Daniel says, his voice trailing off as he stares at the pile of presents for Daniel under the tree. Though it's been two years since the divorce, the sense of loss he feels hasn't diminished by much. And the big question of why still just hangs out there, reverberating in the ether.

"Oh, make sure you let us all talk to him," Gigi says. "I want to tell him we'll be sending off his presents tomorrow. We weren't sure whether he was going to be here or not." Daniel gives her a sharp glance.

"Oh, I'm not saying it was your fault, Dan." She looks at him pleadingly.

Lydia almost shakes her head. She sees how this dynamic between her mother and brother has gathered momentum in recent years. Her need to protect him had begun years ago when Evan passed away and had only grown since Daniel's divorce.

Nothing could remind him more of the apartness from his son than to have to call him on Christmas Day. Daniel wants to go into a room by himself to call. But it's impossible because all these anxious people are hovering over him, waiting to talk to Cole.

Deciding one less female in the room would help to deflate the atmosphere, Lydia walks outside to see what Christmas day in Southport looks like. The brightness and greenness momentarily disorient her, as they did when she first arrived. Carolina wrens flit gaily about the orange-berried Yaupon trees.

She sits on the porch swing, a quaint feature of Southport homes Lydia found inviting and comforting. Swinging back and forth gazing out lazily at the passing world, she feels connected to a rhythm beneath the surface of people, places, and time. She closes her eyes and tilts her head back in a surrender to the air, the sun, the lightness of her body swinging through space. The feeling is familiar, maybe something she had experienced quite recently—or was it in a dream? She squeezes her eyes shut more, as if to see more clearly inside.

Yes, there it was in that dream, spinning around in the field of tall grass, her arms spread wide, head tilted back and face to the sun, feeling so happy, so free!

Lydia hears someone call, though so engaged in her reverie, she's not sure at first where the words are coming from.

"Lydia, the phone is free now if you want to make any calls," her mother says.

The thread of the story is lost now. She reluctantly opens her eyes.

"Oh, that's okay, Mom. I'll make my calls on my cell phone. Thanks anyway."

"If you call your father, please give him my best."

Lydia wonders if her mother really means it, for she never believed her mother cared anything about her dad. But then, she thinks, maybe she does care, and my reaction is part of another family dynamic, this one generated by me: it was all Mother's fault, taking us away from our beloved home and father. This is the first time she's ever doubted this assumption in all the twenty-five years since the divorce. It feels to her like a heavy door has cracked open, letting in a little light.

Ben and George

When Lydia announces her father and Ben are both coming to visit, Gigi seems a little surprised, but not so much that she asks questions about why. Ben had come for visits at other Christmases and for Zipporah's birthdays some years. And George, well, he had always been invited but rarely came. She does wonder a bit why they're coming after Christmas, to which Lydia simply explains they hadn't been able to come before but could for New Year's. Eugenia begins to go into something of a panic about providing for the extra guests, particularly George.

"Don't worry, Mom. I've arranged rooms for both Ben and Dad at the motel I stayed at. You're already doing enough."

"Oh, well, thank you, Lydia. Yes, I guess it's best that they stay there, though I hope they don't think I don't *want* them to stay here."

"No, I'm sure they won't. They, as everyone else who knows you, know how hospitable and gracious you are. You needed worry about that."

Lydia realizes how spontaneously she said something nice about her mother. She was also trying to keep her mother from worrying, but the praise feels genuinely offered.

Eugenia looks at Lydia and blinks once, as if something surprising had forced her eyes to open more.

So anxious that Nans, the name he always called her, might leave this world before he had a chance to see her one more time, Ben got the next available flight from Boston to Wilmington, three days after Christmas. He had wanted to make it for her ninetieth birthday celebration, but work intruded. The last time he saw her was four years ago when he came down for a fishing trip to the Outer Banks and took a side trip to Southport.

Pausing for a moment before knocking on the door, Ben reminds himself not to act anxiously in Gigi's presence, as he promised Lydia he would not reveal what he knew of Zipporah's condition. He was so grateful to be included as the only non-family member in this gathering for Nans. But then, he had always considered himself a part of her family since she was really the one who raised him and spent more time with him when he was very young than his own mother had.

"Oh Benjie, how wonderful to see you," Gigi says as she wraps her arms around him. He usually bristles at being called that name, a childhood moniker he thought he had left long ago. Yet, somehow, it seems almost right coming from Gigi or Nans.

"Hey, man. How's it going?" Daniel greets him with a gesture between a handshake and a hug.

"Well, not too bad. And you?" In the few seconds they exchange glances, an entire short story of all that look and reply mean is conveyed: knowing that they each had experienced the pains of divorce and separation from their children but, like the resilient men they're supposed to be, presenting a cheerful front. And their work, well it was okay, but shouldn't it be somehow more satisfying, the way they always thought their work-obsessed fathers had regarded their jobs?

"Hey, Ben, it's great to see you." Lydia hugs him warmly. "I'll take you over to the motel so you can settle in. I know you want to see Nans, but I think she's sleeping right now. Maybe by the time we come back she'll be up."

George looks out the plane window. It's always so wonderfully relaxing, this being borne high above his daily life of the din of peoples' voices in meetings and on the phone. In flight is the one time and place he can feel removed from it all. How other business executives can sit on a plane with their heads never rising above their papers or computer screens is beyond him.

Yet, despite the years and years that have passed, after a while a persistent memory returns to him: he's standing on the edge of a plane hatch, about to jump down into who knows what danger. Would there be enemies waiting for him hiding behind trees? Would he and his comrades even survive the jump?

George pulls down the window shade, leans his head to the side and closes his eyes.

Being a person of quite formidable will, he trained himself over the years to dream different dreams than he had when he first returned from the war. Before falling into a half-sleep, he easily summons a picture of the land he grew up in, in a verdant, wildflower-filled valley beneath the towering Alps of Switzerland. He hears the cheerful clang of cow bells echoing between the mountains. Then he sees himself gliding down a mountain in the powdery winter snow. How he loved skiing—so elegantly people would say, his long limbs smoothly carving out turns and whooshing down the steep trails. He is not skiing alone, but with someone—yes, his sister. He tries not to think of her, but before he shuts out her memory, he pictures them looking up to the snow-capped mountains, how they felt so small, yet safe and protected.

Dad

Why do I always feel so nervous, Lydia wonders, when I'm about to see my dad? You'd think I was awaiting the arrival of a beau, as they say in the south, whom I want desperately to impress on a first date. Or how nervous I might feel in a room with some dazzlingly brilliant guy I'm intrigued with, who appears aloof and unapproachable, yet tantalizes with an occasional polite smile, and whose soft, brown eyes convey an irresistible tender sadness.

From a green lounge chair at the Riverside Motel, Lydia stares across the Cape Fear River. It surprises her to realize she thinks this way about her father; that she has a yearning for him as if he were the object of an unrequited love—but it *is* like that, isn't it, she thinks, and is there a chance it will ever *not* feel that way?

She then remembers how the muddy banks of the river, with the decomposing life within them, evoked thoughts about the secrets the women in her family kept deeply buried inside them. But what about the secrets her father kept hidden? Compared to the women, his secrets seemed buried in the impenetrable ice of a mighty glacier, words and stories that no force could ever expose.

She hears the motel room door open. George puts down his small suitcase, takes off his jacket and carefully drapes it around the back of the desk chair. Lydia taps on the sliding door, her face slightly pressed against the glass.

He is at first a bit startled, but then realizes it's Lydia and walks over to open the door.

"Lyddie, how are you my dear?" he asks as he hugs her warmly.

She can't help it. She always feels about to cry when she first sees her dad. Why, why? It's so childish, she thinks, but it *is* complicated: she's glad to see him yet already sad to know that when they part they'll both feel something which should have been said hadn't been, and that each will likely remain as much a mystery to the other as before.

"Good, Dad. I wish you'd come into the city more often, so we could go out to lunch or something. It seems kind of crazy. We live only about thirty miles apart," she says half-jokingly, not wanting to sound too serious.

He smiles that slightly sad, inscrutable smile. His hair has thinned and turned a handsome more silvery gray in the year since she's seen him. "I try to avoid going into the city much. You know, I should be retired by now, but I can do most everything from home these days, except for occasional meetings. I don't know what I would do with myself if I retired, honestly. But I promise to make more time to get together in the coming year. So, how is everything at Eugenia's?"

"Okay. I'm so glad you're here, and Nans will be too. It's not going to be long. Ben is already here. He's staying in the next room."

"Ben—oh yes, Dan's friend. It's been a very long time since I've seen him."

"What would you say to a walk along the river?"

"That's exactly what I was thinking. I need to stretch."

They walk along a path across the rough-grassed lawn to the river edge.

"The Cape Fear—doesn't look exactly fearsome, does it Lyddie? Though, as I recall in the film of that name—a really scary movie with Robert Mitchum and Gregory Peck, I think— it was the eerie stillness of the river and the dark, marshy banks that felt almost as menacing as the villain. You imagined hidden secrets were just waiting to be revealed."

Lydia stops for a moment and looks wide-eyed at her dad. "Yes, the hidden secrets in the riverbank. I've been thinking a lot about just that idea, wondering if those hidden things in our past will always haunt us, like in a Greek tragedy or in the idea of karma—that one never really escapes the unexamined past."

"Always the philosophical one, Lyddie," George says, giving her a fatherly pat on top of her head. "Yes, you always were."

They come to the riverbank where a path leads left toward the town landing or right along the bank toward a forest of Spanish moss-laden oaks and cypresses.

"Which way do you want to go, Dad? I bet you want to go toward town—and I suppose you could guess I want to go the other way." She laughs suddenly. "I remember this expression Nans had—maybe it's even the reason I've always been drawn to the woods. She liked to make up stories to tell us when we were little, almost all of them beginning with, 'Once upon a time in the deepy, darky woods.' She also liked telling us she was a witch, which we would laugh at but then she would let down her long, thick hair and make a scary face and we'd almost believe her."

"Zipporah, such a character: sharp, witty, strong-minded," George says. He starts to walk toward the woods. "Strength of character. That's probably the trait I most think of when I think about her. It's so like her not to want everyone to know about her state of health. Strength to the very end."

They walk quietly along the path. As they near the woods, George says, "Well, this certainly looks like a deepy, darky woods. Kind of melancholy, isn't it? Maybe it's the Spanish moss."

"You have to think it's partly how the term Southern Gothic came about. Mysterious, even lugubrious looking. Spanish moss is actually supposed to eventually kill the trees, you know."

"Lugubrious—yes, that's exactly what it's like," he says as they enter the woods and look up at the drooping, epiphytic strands. "One can imagine all sorts of nefarious things happening in a place like this."

"It's interesting how we project our thoughts and feelings onto nature, isn't it?"

"Yes. I guess you're right, Lydia. I haven't thought much about that before, really." He pauses for a moment. "On the plane ride here, I was thinking about being in the Alps as a boy, how that felt. They filled me with a sense of awe and humility, as I remember. Yes, and maybe a sense of protection, too."

"Oh, tell me more, Dad," Lydia says with keen expectation. "I've always wanted to hear more about when you were young in Switzerland."

"Oh, that was a very long time ago, dear. Yes, there are some good stories to tell. I guess I never realized I didn't talk that much about my youth. But I'll try to make up for it, I promise."

She hopes he really means it. But, she thinks, this is always what happens with my family: just when I come upon some hidden treasure from someone's past, it vanishes. No one ever wants to talk about his or her past.

Then, gazing around him at the Spanish moss-laden trees,

he says, "Why don't we head back, Lydia? We probably should be going over to your mother's soon, don't you think? After all, we don't want to linger too long in the deepy, darky woods, do we? Tell me, did that scare you as a little girl when Zipporah would say that?"

"Well, maybe a little. Kids love to be scared, though, don't they? But then, the stories were more fun than scary. In her stories we'd meet odd characters and animals, but not frightening ones. They made me want to go into the woods more. But I don't know about Daniel or Evan. Actually, I don't remember them ever going for long walks in the woods behind our house, the way I did. I do remember they liked to go to that pine grove though."

"Your mother liked to go for walks in those woods, too. She'd ask me to go with her, but I didn't. I'm not exactly sure why." George says these last words as if it is the first time he's ever thought this thought, and that perhaps he'd like to find out the answer.

They emerge from the woods and begin walking back to the motel.

The Missing Hand

Late afternoon light peers through the window, falling upon the shelf across from the end of her bed and illuminating the row of miniature furniture and figures perched there. Zipporah looks upon them with an affectionate smile. They had traveled countless miles with her, had been carefully wrapped in tissue paper and then unwrapped in so many places that, now in her ninth decade, she found it hard to keep track of their journeys. Yet, it was fun to try. Some had been with her as far back as her long ago youth, though most were collected from her time at the museum, miniatures from period dioramas that had been slightly damaged and discarded by the museum conservators.

How glad she is she hasn't had to pack and unpack them for about ten years now; she would worry that, at this point in her life, her once beautiful long fingers, now gnarled and arthritic, would have great difficulty handling such delicate forms without inflicting further damage.

Her favorite pieces were from the late colonial south, given to her as a young girl by her mother. Standing by a grand fireplace made out of tiny bricks was a distinguished-looking man, about three inches high, meticulously dressed in a white ruffled shirt and pale blue vest, perhaps a sea captain, Zipporah had always mused. On the elegantly crafted mahogany dining table were the smallest imaginable blue China plates. Completing the scene, the belle, the captain's wife, stood apart enough to seem quite self-contained yet looked toward him devotedly. She was dressed in a blue satin gown, her auburn hair in a careful bun and porcelain skin so perfect. But alas, upon closer inspection, the face was marred, cracked in more than one place. A gloved hand was also missing.

Zipporah's particular fondness for them was understandable since her grandmother was a young woman in this time, just after the Civil War, and had lived not far from here in a colonial mansion with her grandfather who, in fact, had been a prosperous sea captain. Yet her fondness for the belle had increased immeasurably after it had been broken.

Zipporah knew he had not meant to damage the figurine; rarely in their frequent impassioned arguments would he express his anger physically. But this one time he had, just before they had separated. When he had thrown his shoe at the nearby wall, of all the delicate miniatures on the shelf, only the belle—as if it were a tiny image of Zipporah herself—fell from the force.

Continuing to gaze upon the figurine, Zipporah thinks how she, too, had suffered her share of falls and breaks, and had always picked herself up, had always carried on, her head held high. Strength of character—I guess that's what people called it, she thinks. Yet now, as she contemplates the missing hand on the figurine, she begins to see something else, a thought that had risen to the surface of her mind before, but that she had always pushed down. Maybe, she thinks. the time has finally come to let those thoughts come up; to let that proud chin drop.

Sure, I had been strong, forged a life for myself and young

daughter, north in New York, away from my husband I left brooding in the south, she thinks. And after eight years, I at last answered his plea to return. I really had never stopped loving him either. Then, one dark day only a few months after our joyous reunion, he fell dead of a heart attack at the still young age of thirty-eight. It was the hardest on poor little Gigi—she had adored her daddy so and for the first time in eight years had been truly happy again.

Zipporah shakes her head slowly in a gesture of sad yet relieved recognition: What, for God's sake, was I trying to prove, and to whom exactly? I forged ahead alright, but it was as if, as if—her eyes fix upon the belle's missing hand—it had been only with one hand!

She turns her gaze to a photo on her bureau of Gigi as a girl of about eight. Yes, I led, firmly, even sternly—God knows I was only trying to be the strong mother in the face of all that had gone wrong, all that had been missed! But God also knows we need two hands to properly guide and—oh, yes—to completely embrace a child.

Zipporah allows herself a quiet cry.

There's a knock on the door. She pulls out the tissue tucked into her sleeve and pats the pale skin under her eyes.

"Come on in but beware of the old witch."

"Nans! How great it is to see you!"

"Benjie—I guess I shouldn't call you that anymore. My, look at you! You sure look swell. Still got that cute head of curly hair, I'm glad to see."

"Well, you look good too, Nans." He leans over and gently picks up her frail hand folded on her lap.

"Now, don't you be tellin' fibs. You know I look about as swell as a slug."

He laughs. "You know, I don't think I've heard that word 'fib' since I last saw you. It sounds so much less damning than lie, doesn't it? I may not hear the word spoken by others, but after all these years, I have to say I hear it in my mind more often than you can imagine. It's only one of the many words and lessons from you I carry with me still."

"Oh, poor you, having an old witch like me hounding you to kingdom come." She scrunches up her face.

"Well, I'm sure glad you're here, Benjie." She lifts her other hand placing it on top of his. "I have plans for us while we're all gathered together. When Lydia's and Dan's dad gets here, I want us to visit a special place I used to go as a little girl, down in the town park."

"I think George has just arrived."

"Oh goodie. The sooner we can go the better." With the sudden realization of what she means, Ben places his other hand on top of hers and squeezes his eyes shut trying to hold back the tears.

"Oh now, don't you fret too much, sweet potatoes. I really am ready to go. I've been here probably too long as it is. Nobody likes it when you stay too long at the party, you know."

"Maybe that's true of most people, but not you, Nans, not you." He thinks of his mother, the years he took care of her after her stroke; how he felt she indeed had lived too long.

With their hands layered upon each other resting on Zipporah's lap, he feels a well of love rise up to his heart.

Lovers' Oak

They're all standing in a semi-circle around the enormous tree, their eyes staring in wonder. They look up to see where the tree ends but what commands their attention more is the astonishing horizontal nature of the thing. Its massive trunk is impressive enough, yet it's the maze of twisting, intertwining branches and vines that appear, at least to Lydia, to want to enfold them all in its dense brown and green realm.

Zipporah alone looks on smilingly, as if encountering a dear friend after too long being apart. Leaning heavily on her cane, she walks up to the tree and touches its trunk with her free hand. She feels along the deeply ridged bark, perhaps finding a sense of kinship in its aged exterior. Her fingers continue their searching, which makes Eugenia begin to worry if her mother's eccentricity had progressed into serious strangeness.

"Ah, here it is," Zipporah says excitedly, looking to the left side of the tree. "And after all these years. Hot diggity dog!"

She traces her fingers over a spot on the huge trunk, then turns to face everyone.

"Effie and I used to love to climb this tree when we lived in Southport as youngsters. We carved our names into the trunk with my pen knife when we were maybe ten years old.

Effie used to tease me that I was too much like the boys 'cause I carried a pen knife, adored climbing trees and goin' fishing, things proper little girls didn't do in my day, though I guess that's what he liked about me. It was my idea to carve our names; then he surprised me and proceeded to carve a heart around them."

Zipporah leans harder on her cane, looking down at a spot slightly in front of her where some of the tree's giant roots had pushed up out of the ground in graceful arcs, as if to show they were not just of the solid earth but of the sky and spirit world, too.

"Now, everyone called it Lovers' Oak, so I thought at first, oh, he's just carving this heart 'cause he wants to be part of the tradition, not that he means anything by it. But when he was finished, he held my hands, which must have taken a lot of courage for a ten-year-old boy, and looked at me so intently with those knowing eyes that it almost scared me, and said, 'I know we sometimes fight like the dickens, but I also know it hurts when I'm waiting to see you again.'"

Zipporah shakes her head and smiles wryly. "Lord knows, that was the truth for the rest of our married life, short and fitful as it was."

She looks up now toward the highest branches of the tree looming over her like a protective god. "It sure is amazing how sometimes we can know such truths in our hearts, fleetingly. But then some kind of force in us keeps us fighting against that light, pulling us downward to something dark inside, so that we end up blaming the very thing we're struggling to understand, to embrace, to love."

Zipporah pauses. Everyone has shifted their stunned gaze from the tree to her. Lydia thinks that Zipporah has always had a touch of this Oracle at Delphi about her. But standing there now, Druid-like in front of this primordial tree, she doesn't have the usual self-effacing tone when pronouncing a surprising truth, which often would be followed by laughing at herself so as not to appear too self-important. Now she's looking at each person gathered around, her shining dark eyes inquiring yet challenging at the same time. Her gaze comes to settle on Eugenia.

"I want you to know, Gigi, that I always loved your father, even when we were apart. And that I'm sorry I took you away from him because I think if I hadn't been so doggone—it was more than stubborn, more like asininely thick-headed and impulsively proud—we would have stayed together and worked it out somehow. And I want to apologize also for being so God-awful strict and just plain witchy-bitchy. I can see you probably never blossomed into the person you could have because I simply didn't allow you to. Forgive me, though I know this is probably more than even the good Lord can forgive."

Zipporah leans more heavily upon her cane, as if the gravity of her confession is pulling her downward. Her face contorts with what appears to be pain. With some effort, she turns her face upward through the oak's high branches to the fragments of blue sky; as she does, the pained expression vanishes, and her childlike smile reappears.

"Thank you God for all these people here I love and for whom my fervent wish is that you can help them realize whatever they need to. Thank you for such creations as this tree that help bring us closer to your truth. And thank you for what has been, despite my grumbling and occasional swearing at you, a quite marvelous life." And then she falls to the ground upon the arcing roots of the great tree known as Lovers' Oak.

The Broken Belle and the Dream

Zipporah had left instructions to have her ashes scattered in the Cape Fear River, and some, discreetly, underneath Lovers' Oak. The service had been simple, in keeping with her wishes. It was to be more celebration than mourning, which it was, with family members and dear friends, like Ben, sharing fond memories and reflections. For the scattering of the ashes, Daniel and Lydia arrange for a boat to take everyone down the Cape Fear. A more obscure instruction was to have one of her beloved miniatures, the elegant southern belle with the cracked face and missing hand, tossed into the river with the ashes.

As she re-reads her mother's last wishes, Eugenia sees that this last part, about the miniature, was probably written after everything else. It was in an erratic, almost indecipherable script, unlike the careful, though somewhat wobbly, handwriting of the rest of the letter. She begins to ponder her mother's dignified handwriting and how she always wished she had handwriting like that rather than her awkwardly slanting, embarrassing left-handed script. Her mother had agreed with the teachers, who back then thought there was something terribly wrong with natural left-handedness and engaged in vigorous efforts to transform such afflicted children into becoming right-handed. But their efforts weren't successful with Eugenia, which she knew was just one more of her mother's disappointments in her.

Eugenia lifts her eyes as a solitary tear falls onto the page blurring the word "missing." She looks in front of her to the shelf of miniatures and sees the belle of the missing hand. Her mother's last words, "Please forgive me though I know this is probably more than even the good Lord can forgive," come back to her, as they had a hundred times over.

"How can it be that after sixty-seven years my mother apologized to me, and for just about everything?" she whispers, as if addressing the miniature belle. She notices the belle's arms are outstretched with the one remaining gloved hand palm up in a gesture suggesting graciousness. But Eugenia begins to observe something else in that gesture, something denoting compassion and forgiveness. Even the belle's face, tilting to the side, possesses a smile that appears completely without guile, as completely open as the arms and hands.

Eugenia reaches for the figurine and holds it tightly in both hands, almost in a pose of prayer. She has a sudden sense of air expanding and rising from the center of her body to the top of her head, a feeling of opening up and releasing. The words "Forgive, forgive!" come rushing up to her mind. Yes, yes, but the missing hand, she wonders, the missing hand! She cannot know how the belle had been broken—that in a fit of anger at her mother, her father had thrown something that caused it to fall—but Eugenia now knows that something in Zipporah had broken when she left him, and that despite pushing ahead, proudly, stubbornly, as she had said under the old oak tree, it was as if it had been only with one hand.

The boat motors along so slowly and quietly and the water is so still, it seems to everyone they are in a sort of dream. Their hands resting lightly upon the aged mahogany railing, they gaze below at the opaque surface of the Cape Fear River as it parts in the yacht's stately passing. The antique boat Daniel had rented for the occasion—so thoughtfully, a beautifully restored 1930 Elco yacht, the same that Zipporah's husband Effingham had owned—casts a spell of its own, transporting them into another time. The captain of the vessel is dressed in a navy blazer, bow tie, cream colored linen pants, and a Panama hat to add to the period ambiance. Along the riverbank, nothing disrupts the illusion of the past either, dense woods of cypress and Spanish moss-covered oaks stretching on and on.

Lifting her gaze from the river, Gigi stares at the captain. She doesn't know why she's staring at him. Yes, he looks very handsome in his attire, she thinks, but it's more than that: something about him reminds her of someone else. Her mind scans the recent past, the not so recent past, but she can't retrieve it.

As she closes her eyes and tries not to think but rather gives herself over to the sound of the water, the drifty feeling of the boat and the smell of the cypress trees, it suddenly comes to her: the captain looks like the figure in her dream of about a week ago, the man on the riverbank waving to her as she drifts down the river, farther and farther away. "Goodbye Gigi, now don't be afraid, and don't you forget you'll always be my best girl," she remembers him saying. And then she waves back, trying to be brave, fighting back the tears. She drifts around a bend, the man no longer in sight.

Eugenia now realizes the dream was of course about her father. But there was something else that happened in the dream after the sadness, something that made her feel light and happy again. Yes, she began painting pictures in the boat, of the trees along the river, the wildflowers and birds, and, she recalls, even an amusing crocodile peering above the water.

First Gigi, then Lydia and Daniel, scatter into the river Zipporah's ashes which they each have in tiny urns. George and Aunt Virginia, a nephew and cousins from Michigan who came for the ceremony as Zipporah had wished, then Ben, scatter theirs. Gigi still has the figurine, which she is to throw into the river too, as her mother instructed.

She asks everyone to gather in a circle. She holds up the miniature and tells everyone what she has come to realize about her mother, from the words spoken under the oak tree and from contemplating this broken figurine. She tells them about the dream of her father, and that among her most cherished memories with him as a little girl were boat trips in his Elco yacht going down a beautiful river in Florida that led out to the ocean. Then she reminds them of her mother's last words under the oak tree: that she hoped with God's help and the help of his creations—the great trees, lands and rivers of the world—everyone gathered around would come to realize something they needed to for themselves.

"It sometimes seems to take a lifetime to realize important things, and it's been almost that for me," Gigi says, sighing deeply. Then she closes her eyes and grips the figure more tightly. "I'll have no more bitter thoughts about choices you made concerning me, mother. And I offer my deepest gratitude for the good example you were in so many ways, and for your wisdom that I think I'll be more able to appreciate now. Lastly, I do believe you and father will be happy together again." Eugenia then gently tosses the little broken belle into the river.

Everyone watches as if transfixed by the ripples flowing out from the fallen figurine. Lydia feels those ripples move out beyond the river, farther and farther out into the universe.

Ripples

As she looks out at the night sky through the small windows of her attic room, Lydia thinks about her mother's words just before she tossed the figurine overboard. How extraordinary they were, how they seemed to Lydia to have emanated from a being wholly unlike the one she had known all her life—even as if her mother had been briefly possessed by a spirit from another world. Maybe, in fact, she had been: by the ghost of her mother Zipporah, in the form of the figurine.

But was it just a brief moment without any lasting meaning, or would her mother be different, Lydia wonders? And what about the bitterness toward Zipporah that Eugenia confessed to having all her life? Had that fermented into the damaged fruit of her feelings toward her own daughter, me? Yes, probably, she thinks, but it seems too facile an explanation to be the whole truth.

The stars seem so very far away through the window, yet the more Lydia contemplates them the closer they appear, as if they were being held in a great embrace. She recalls the ripples of water formed from the thrown miniature earlier that day, how she felt those ripples encircle her and others on the boat, and then move out into the air beyond; those circles created from the power of her grandmother's words: that with the help of God's creations everyone gathered around would come to realize something they needed to for themselves.

God's creations, God's creations, Lydia thinks. Yes! Hadn't it been through her grandmother's memories, experiences and youthful love associated with an old oak tree that her revelations had come? And for her mother, hadn't it been through memories of being with her beloved father on a boat in a river, revealed in her dream and then on the Cape Fear that day, that her shattering insights had come?

Lydia closes her eyes. What is that touchstone for me in this world, she whispers prayerfully?

Like a fast rewinding film, images of favorite places rush by in her mind: the magical wildness of Manhattan's Fort Tryon Park and, in its midst, the Gregorian chant-filled halls of the Cloisters where she spent almost every Sunday afternoon; further back in time, the bucolic beauty of her college campus dotted with handsome old stone buildings in the Hudson Valley; even further back, the shining green-shuttered home of her childhood with its seemingly endless gardens of phlox and lilies she helped her mother tend; and lastly, she sees the meadow—the meadow, beyond the house and beyond the hill, that she loved to run through and sometimes felt the spirit to dance in.

She opens her eyes, recalling the recurring dream she had of dancing in a meadow and of feeling a pure joy, reveling in a sense of beauty and freedom—as if they were one and the same thing; this feeling that seemed to be directed from both within and without.

Lydia closes her eyes again. Like a healing rain, tears wash over her eyes. Oh my God! That is what I had really wanted to do with my life! I must have buried it so thoroughly that it only appeared in dreams. The ballet classes my mother took me to.

I loved the movements, the grace and precision of them, but did not feel I had the talent, nor the right body. And, though my mother was kind enough to introduce me to the classes, I thought she didn't believe I would actually ever distinguish myself as a dancer.

But was it really so much she who didn't believe in me or me who didn't believe in me, Lydia wonders? Don't we remember many things about our childhood through the self-centered lens of a child and miss much of what may have been lying beneath the surface? Isn't it true that a mother's ardent instinct to nurture often lies underneath what we perceive, or misperceive, as children?

Lydia again recalls the image she had looking out over the Cape Fear River on her first night in Southport; how she imagined that the secret life breeding and decomposing in the muddy banks just below the shining surface was a metaphor for people like her grandmother and mother who, belying their vibrant personalities, kept so many secrets tightly bound inside; secrets that, like the tiny creatures in the river's muddy banks, with time decompose, but never, never really die, rather become part of the rich layer of matter that broadens and deepens over the years. Some of this rich matter pushes new thoughts, new forms through to the life-giving air above, but much of it remains hidden below and forever unknown.

As if suddenly she's seeing through layers of silty water that have clouded her vision, she realizes now that it's a metaphor for her, too. By way of one of God's beautiful creations—a meadow—some of the rich buried matter in her life has at last pushed through to the life-giving air above.

New Year's Resolutions

Lydia carefully cuts the string beans into neat julienne pieces. Her mother takes down pots from the cast iron rack above the stove, but noticeably, without the clanging noise she usually made while doing it.

In the evening, family members gather around the table one more time, for New Year's Eve dinner; relatives from Michigan and Ben had to return home with other engagements for the holiday.

"Happy New Year," everyone chimes in at the same time, lifting their glasses in a toast.

As she looks at the candleflame, Lydia begins to imagine relevés and pirouettes in the flickering light. When she pictures herself dancing in a meadow, she smiles, knowing now where the once-mysterious meadow is in the world and what it means. She feels somehow different, less anxious, less like she's eternally waiting for something in the vague future and more like, almost magically, a piece of the puzzle of her life had been found and fit into place.

"I wish Nans were here," Lydia says. "I would tell her what a gift she gave us by saying what she did underneath that oak tree. On the boat yesterday, Mom reminded us of that gift. And now I, too, have realized something. As long as I can remember, I've had a recurring dream about dancing in a meadow. Last night I finally understood that that meadow was up beyond the house where we lived on Long Island, a place I used to love to go and where I felt something wonderful: a visceral sense of being a beautiful being in a beautiful world; of not being an isolated, lonely entity, as I usually felt, but a complete and integral part of the world. Sometimes, being there moved me to dance and I imagined myself as a dancer.

"I buried that wish, mostly under thoughts of being practical, I think. Of course, I'll never be a dancer at this point in my life, but I can take classes, and maybe, even if I'm not dancing in a meadow, I'll have some of that wonderful feeling again."

Usually when her daughter talked in this philosophical vein, particularly when it was personal, Eugenia would look exasperated. Instead, they share a smile.

"Well, that's great, Lydia," Eugenia says warmly. "I remember how you loved dance. It will probably be very good for you to start dancing again.

"Your story, Lydia, reminds me of a part of the dream— the one I told you all, about the boat and the river—I didn't mention before: at the end of the dream, as I drifted down the river, away from my father, I began to paint watercolors of the trees and flowers, even a crocodile I saw in the water. And then I was happy again."

"That's so interesting, Mom. I remember how you appreciated art and seemed to know a lot about artists in history. I always thought maybe you had wanted to be one yourself," Lydia offers. "Maybe there's a message in the dream: you should take up painting."

"Yes, that was what I was thinking, too!" Eugenia says, her eyes lighting up.

"Well, well," Aunt Gina says cheerfully. "Now we have a dancer and a painter in the family. We did have some good singers, both of my older sisters, Lolly and Zipporah's mom, Cecilia."

"But doesn't everyone see what a big deal all of this is?" Lydia asks, excitement rising in her voice. "Remember at Christmas dinner when we had that discussion about the word humus and the idea of humility: that the earth is what links us all together? This gift that Nans gave us is about discovering a link to our past that has its roots in the natural world, a place that may lead us to some sort of revelation about ourselves. I have my meadow and Mom has her river and Nans had her oak tree. Maybe there's a place in your past, Gina, and maybe in Dan's, and in Dad's too," she says as she looks from one face to the other.

Gina squints, straining to see something in the vague distance. George furrows his brow in deep thought as he looks slightly downward and Daniel shifts uncomfortably in his chair.

"Sounds a little fuzzy, Lydia. A little like that transcendental stuff I remember reading back in college—Emerson and Thoreau," Daniel says lightheartedly.

"Yes, Dan. Among my very favorite writers. But the thing is, this isn't just theory or something from a book. This has happened. This is real!"

"You know sugar, when you have as much to remember as I do, everything kind of swirls together," Gina says, almost in a whisper, her gnarled hands and fingers now moving in front of her, as if trying to give form to what was in her mind. "But there are some memories that just jump out of that swirl, like one of me as a very young mother on the shore over at Oak Island, staring out across that endless water and wondering if my husband Harry would ever come back from the First

World War, and thank the Lord, he did. Then he went into the fishing business here and was caught in a hurricane off the Outer Banks and was gone forever.

"The ocean had become a place of sadness, so I never wanted to go to the ocean again. My son Gordon went into the Navy in the Second World War, and came back, but then wanted to go into the Merchant Marines. I begged him not to, to do anything but that, that he had been lucky to have come back from the war, but he wanted to go. Then, his ship was lost at sea in a storm."

Gina takes a deep breath. "When we were on the boat the other day and I listened to the water lapping on the sides as we scattered Zipporah's ashes, I thought of how sad, and even angry, too, I had been for them leaving me. But then the sound of the water brought me back to an even earlier time when I loved the shore more than any other place and imagined the ocean as holding out the highest of adventure and possibility.

"Going back in my mind to that feeling, I suddenly had this bright thought I don't think I ever had before in my ninety-eight years, or at least as clearly: that part of the love for loved ones is to let them go answer their calls in life and that, whatever those calls may be, they will always contain both adventure and sadness."

Gina looks upward, as if at an unseen presence. "Maybe now, after all these years, I'll have more peace of mind."

Everyone looks at Gina, their eyes slightly misty, even Dan's and George's. Sitting next to her, Lydia holds her hand. On Gina's left side, Eugenia holds the other hand.

"Thank you for that powerful, amazing story, Aunt Gina," Lydia says.

After an extended pause, Lydia continues. "Now, I have a proposition for you, Dan. How about you and I go back to the house on Long Island to check it out. See if my meadow is still there. And maybe there's something there you'd like to find."

Daniel is completely surprised by this. "Well, Lydia, I've never thought about going back there. I don't know. It's been so many years."

"Oh, please, Dan. I think it would be good for us. It would be fun to go on a little trip together, too."

Lydia expects her mother to give her that Daniel-protector gaze. But instead, her raised eyebrows and slight smile seem to Lydia encouraging gestures.

"Okay, well maybe," Dan says tentatively.

"What about you, Dad?" Lydia asks. "Is there someplace you want to go?"

George stares at the candle flame. The shape of the flame brings to his mind the image of a mountain peak. "Well, if there is a place I'd like to go back to it would be Switzerland. As you all know, I grew up in the Alps. Once in a while I see it in my memory. I did go back a couple of times, but just on business trips to Geneva and Zurich. I never went off to the countryside near Zurich where I grew up."

No one knows quite what to say. Then George adds, "So, it might be good to go. What about you and Dan come with me? I think I had always wanted to take you two but somehow it never happened."

Daniel and Lydia look at each other. "Wow, that would be really great, Dad," Daniel says.

"Yes, absolutely. That would be fantastic," Lydia chimes in.

"I think it's a wonderful idea," Eugenia adds. "A trip of the three of you together. A good new year's resolution."

"But first, let's go to Long Island, Dan. We could even meet Dad out there."

"No, I think it would be best if you two go without me,"

George says. "I'll plan our trip to Switzerland. How about going in the spring?"

"I'll have some vacation time around Easter," Lydia says.

"Yes, that would be good for me too," Dan adds.

Lydia raises her wine glass. "Let's all make another toast to the new year, to new beginnings and old places."

Ralph

"Hey Lydia. You must have had a good vacation," Ralph says as he's passing by her workstation the Monday morning after she returned home. "You look...happy."

"Oh, hi Ralph. Yes, I had an amazing time. Lots of good things happened. Family stuff." She decides not to mention her grandmother's death.

"And what about you?"

"Yes. I spent Christmas with my folks and sister's family. Then went to St. John for some sun. Well, I'm a little late so I better get to work. See you around."

"Yes, for sure."

Well, imagine that, Lydia thinks. I'm at work and I look happy! As she scrolls down the page she's editing on the computer, she doesn't feel that same sense of being half somewhere else. It's as if, she thinks, in my mind I had always been looking for a lost and forgotten something and I've finally found it. I can do this job; I can even maybe enjoy it. And after work today I'm going to my first dance class!

"Thank you, Harold. Oh, I almost forgot," she says to the doorman as he opens the door. She reaches into her purse and pulls out a small package. "I wanted to bring you something from North Carolina. I tried it for the first time while I was there. It's really tasty. Maybe you remember it from when you lived there?"

"Oh my, my! Yaupon tea. Why, thank you Miss Lydia. Yes indeed, my folks used to gather the leaves and make the tea. Coffee was kind of expensive and you could get just as good a buzz from the Yaupon tea anyway, especially with a little molasses or honey in it. And thank you for those chocolates you gave me for Christmas. You know, you don't have to give me presents."

"It's not a matter of have to—I like to. Of everyone in this place, you are one of my favorites, Harold. Truly."

Underneath his mocha-toned skin, she could see the hint of a blush. "Well, I'm off to my first dance class, Harold. I'm so excited!"

The studio is uptown on Broadway, conveniently just around the corner from her apartment on Columbus Avenue. In trying to decide what kind of class to take from the dizzying array of choices available, she decided that it might be best to go back to the basics of ballet, then she could branch out into modern and ethnic dances.

The studio is spacious and airy with lofty ceilings and huge arched windows looking out over Broadway. Putting on her black ballet slippers, leotard, and tights in the changing area, Lydia has a strange rush of feeling, as if she's whirring through time, backwards but at the same time forwards.

The teacher, Nadia Beech, is a woman of about forty to forty-five, Lydia guesses. A former New York City Ballet dancer, she's elegant and lovely in the way only dancers can be, gorgeous bones in her face and body, blond hair in a ponytail. The class specified for women and men thirty-five to forty-five, so Lydia knows she won't feel intimidated by some ridiculously agile and flexible twenty-somethings, though some students would surely be a lot more experienced than she.

Stretching at the bar—oh, how fantastic this feels, Lydia thinks, as if my body has been crying out for this. Even the strain feels good! Nadia walks by each dancer, positioning the arms of most of them, including Lydia's.

"Now all of you, please remember arms, arms, arms are as important as legs! Where the strength is in the legs, the grace is in the arms. Let them flow, flow and follow." Her voice is strong but has a soft, encouraging quality.

Lydia is momentarily self-conscious, for her body remembers that her arms are what she had the most trouble with as a girl in ballet classes. She could point her toes okay and had strong legs, but the arms—what to do with the arms? In some way they never felt as attached to her body as her legs. They would do things she didn't necessarily want them to do.

But then she remembers how she felt in the meadow when she danced. Suddenly her arms would feel released from something constricting them. Maybe it was the wind through the tall grass or maybe a bird flying overhead that unbound them? She closes her eyes and imagines these things, hoping her arms will respond.

With one hand on the bar and the other in an arc over their head, dancers are instructed, with Nadia demonstrating, to put their feet into first position, second, third, fourth, then fifth. How perfect each seems in its orderliness and progression, Lydia thinks. And how liberating orderliness can feel!

Walking home after class along Broadway before turning down Columbus, Lydia feels a lightness in her step; the sounds, lights and faces all around have an aliveness and almost symphonic beauty she didn't often feel in the city. She usually avoids looking at faces, but not this evening. Even the most serious and frowning faces she cannot help but smile at.

Just before arriving at her apartment, her cell phone rings. She doesn't recognize the number but answers it anyway.

"Hello, Lydia? It's Ralph."

"Oh, hi. What a surprise. I'm just getting home."

"Do you want me to call back?"

"No, no. That's fine."

"I was wondering if you'd like to go out for dinner sometime, maybe tomorrow."

She's momentarily speechless. The handsome, dashing Ralph asking *me* out?

"Um, sure I'd like that."

"Great. So, I know you live uptown off Broadway. There's a nice little French bistro on Broadway and 76th. Do you know it?"

"Yes, it happens to be one of my favorites."

"Terrific. Shall we meet there at seven-thirty?"

"Okay. See you then."

Inside her apartment, after shedding her coat, she pours herself a glass of wine, normally not something she did upon just arriving home. But she's in a celebratory mood from her dance class and a date with Ralph.

Sitting on the couch with her legs propped up on the coffee table, she takes a sip, her eyes wide with unexpected happiness. Something is happening, something wonderful but she didn't know whether to believe it was anything that would last beyond tomorrow.

I've worked with Ralph for about two years, she reflects, and suddenly he asks me out? Yes, he said he thought I looked happy today—maybe *that* was it. I guess I had always looked unhappy, which is understandably a turnoff for most people.

Last time she had a date with someone at the magazine was about three months ago. And that did not go well. He was one of the many oh-so-impressed-with-himself people who works there, who talked with a kind of phony British accent and dropped a lot of names—at a party in the Hamptons with so-and-so, a chic bar in midtown where he hung out with so-and-so. She couldn't wait for the evening to end.

After eating some leftovers in the fridge, Lydia starts to run a hot bath, knowing it will help to ease what she expects will be an aching body from the dance class. Feeling more relaxed than she had in a very long time, she tucks herself into bed and soon finds herself falling asleep, dreaming of dancing in a meadow.

Complementary Shades of Blue

Blue eyes and black hair—such an intriguing contrast of light and dark, transparency and hiddenness, Lydia thinks as she tries hard not to be obviously staring across the small dining table at Ralph. Maybe he'll just think I'm very interested in what he's saying. Except I think I'm still staring long after he's finished talking. Okay, get a grip now. Look down at your yummy-looking butterscotch crème brûlée and stare at that for a while.

"Umm, delicious," she says after taking a small spoonful.

"Yes, really good. Funny we ordered the same thing," Ralph rejoins, smiling and looking intently into her eyes. A moment goes by.

"I wanted to tell you first, Lydia. I'm going back to school to get my architectural degree. I was a year away from graduating, but was running out of money, so decided to go to work. I've saved enough money now, more than enough really. I was getting comfortable just writing about architecture, and now I'm getting bored. It all sounds like so much puffery sometimes, as we seem to agree," he says with a little laugh. "I think actually creating the architecture will be a welcome relief. So, very soon now, I'll be leaving."

Lydia is so surprised, her dessert-laden spoon remains in a state of suspended animation inches from her mouth.

"Yes, that makes perfect sense. You must follow your dreams, as wise people say. I'm really happy for you, Ralph," she says, probably not too convincingly. Yes, I am happy, she thinks, but also sad. This will probably be the end of my dates with Ralph. Yep, just as I thought. One great date and end of story.

"You look so much happier at work since you've been back from vacation, Lydia."

"Well, I found something in my past I connected with that has to do with dance. And now I'm taking dance classes, so I hope to keep the good vibe going. Working at the magazine is what it is."

"Dance. That sounds great. Maybe you can find some sort of work in the field. What about writing for a dance magazine?"

Lydia stares at Ralph for a few moments, not because of his hair and eyes but because she hadn't thought of what he just suggested.

"That's a great idea, Ralph. Yes, I think I might very well look into that." She smiles broadly. She doesn't feel the sting so much of him leaving the magazine, thinking soon she might, too.

"Well, this has been a great evening, Lydia," he says as he finishes paying the check. He looks into her eyes.

"You have really lovely eyes, you know. Sort of like the sky with a light morning mist."

Lydia doesn't know what to say. She always thought of the color of her eyes as washed-out.

"Oh, well, thank you, Ralph. *You* are the one with the gorgeous eyes. I hope you don't mind me staring at you, which I think I do too obviously. I have always found black hair and blue eyes so striking."

"Very kind of you. Well, we will, I hope, get to look at each other's eyes more often in the future." He reaches across the table and holds her hand—oh, so gently, yet intently—for a moment, looking even further into her eyes.

"Yes, I hope so too."

The Pine Grove

As he's driving to the airport in Savannah, Daniel passes by a long line of Georgia pines on both sides of the highway. He feels slightly disoriented, as he recalls he did when driving by a such a forest of trees on his way to North Carolina. Their brooding darkness and sort of sad branches at the crown, which seem too small and scant in proportion to the great height of the tree, convey an eeriness he can't quite grasp.

He's relieved to finally leave the trees and come to the outskirts of the airport where he's comforted by acres of motels and fast-food restaurants lining the road.

Once aloft in the plane, he closes his eyes and thinks of his last weekend with Cole. It had been Cole's birthday and, having missed Christmas with him, Daniel made up for it with an extra-celebratory couple of days: ice-skating at an indoor rink, going to the movies, a museum, out to a restaurant Cole liked, and just hanging out at home watching a basketball game together. It was the best time; Daniel loves nothing more than to spend time with his son. He wonders if it would seem as special if he saw Cole all the time; hard to say, but remembering the first eight years when they were still together as a family, seeing his son every day always felt like it brought with it some new, powerful.... His mind searches for the answer. What was it? A sort of *potential* of being maybe. Life in the making. A sparkle and breath that animated the world.

Soon, the plane lands at JFK where Lydia will meet him then drive out to Long Island to visit the old homestead. Since making that promise on New Year's Day, Daniel has gone from feeling somewhat intrigued to almost repelled by it. But now it's going to happen so he's decided he'll be as amenable as possible, for his sister's sake at least, as it seems to mean so much to her.

"Have you been out here at all over the years, Lydia?" Daniel asks as they're driving on the Long Island Expressway about an hour from their childhood hometown.

"Well, not to Smithtown. I've gone out to the east end of the island in the summers, mostly to Greenport on the north shore, and a few times to Montauk on the south shore. Maybe I thought it would just be too sad to go back home. Too sad because it would bring me back to leaving it the way we did, leaving it and Dad and moving away with Mom. And sad on the other hand because it will be so changed it won't be the way I remember it.

"But remembering the beautiful meadow beyond the woods, and how it's been such an important key to unlocking a hidden door in my life, has made me feel differently about going back. I want to see and feel the place, even if it has changed, and maybe even if it's not there at all. I want to feel that it *was* there, to physically connect with that part of my past."

Daniel looks out the right side window. Cars stretching four lanes wide. Not a tree to be seen anywhere. "I'm really glad for you, Lydia. And I can see why you want to go back. But for me, it feels like going back too far. I've got so much to deal with in the more recent past, you know. Stuff I'm still trying to figure out. Why did it happen? Is it at all possible we could be together again? It's been two years but I still think about it almost fifty percent of the time."

"Yes, but you know Dan, we often don't know where answers will come from. Sometimes they don't come from us trying to figure things out. They come through another door. Through the heart and through the body. We store memories in our bodies as well as our minds, you know, and if we're in the right place at the right time and tune in to ourselves, we might hear the answer."

"Oh, Lydia. There you go with your airy talk. Well, you know, I'm a facts and numbers sort of guy."

"But you know reason doesn't work all the time. Not to imply you haven't been trying, but don't you think you might have figured things out about your marriage if that were the only way? There could be something farther back in your life, something you can't yet recall. This is what happened to me, but I learned it through a dream, and through the stories of our grandmother and mother. Maybe it will happen for you when we go back to our home."

Daniel stares stubbornly ahead, finally saying grudgingly, "I doubt it, but I guess it can't hurt to try."

When they reach the town, nothing is recognizable—not one storefront, not one name. Their father's modern glass and concrete building, built in the late 1950s and the first of its kind in the town, a structure which seemed because of its size and imposing form it would be there forever, had completely vanished. The five-and-ten-cent store next door, where they had bought Babe Ruths and Snickers, was gone too, the entire Main Street now a big thoroughfare with shopping centers on either side.

Once they drive outside of town, in what was quaintly called

The Village of the Branch where colonial houses with white picket fences reigned, one boasting that George Washington had slept there, things felt a bit more familiar. The area had been deemed historically significant and was supposed to be preserved in perpetuity, though only a few amongst the dozen or so houses were left intact, and others had been modified into professional buildings.

As Lydia and Daniel approach the driveway to their old home, they both experience a jolt of reality. The driveway is still quite long, but years ago one couldn't see the house from the road because the driveway was lined with trees and bushes and wildflowers. Now, there's nothing growing on either side, and they can see the house from the road. They turn to each other, their eyes wide.

"I don't know, Lydia. Do we really want to go down there?" Daniel's strong, baritone voice sounds a little quaky.

Trying to cancel out her brother's fear with as much reassuring authority as she can muster, Lydia responds, "Of course. We are here. It is different, but we should expect that. It's been twenty-five years, right?"

"Yeah, and someone else owns it now, and will probably not be thrilled for us to be dropping in for a visit."

"We won't try to go in. I just want to walk into the woods in the back if it's still there. The house doesn't matter that much. Besides, I bet it's like other houses in the area, a professional building now, so we'll just park and then go for a walk."

Lydia drives down the driveway slowly, feeling as if she's entering a sort of dreamscape or different dimension. When they get to the house, they see a white sign saying Branch Medical Offices, with three M.D.s' names listed below it. There's an entrance along the side, and a paved parking lot to the right of that. The house appears pretty much the same, a white colonial with green shutters, though there are fewer windows in front than when they lived there. They assume the screened porch on the other side, where they used to love watching summer lighting storms, had been removed, too.

They park in the lot and gaze off to the right and see that the woodland, part of the original ten acres of property, is miraculously still there.

"Maybe it's stranger that the house looks almost the same than if it were very different," Lydia says, in a whisper. "This way, we can imagine ourselves still here."

Daniel is silent. So many feelings and images of the past flood into his brain, he doesn't know what to say.

"Well, shall we go for a little walk? I can't believe the woods are still here," Lydia says excitedly.

They get out of the car, see a faint remnant of a path and begin walking. It's the middle of March, and spring is just beginning to appear, the buds of the mountain laurel barely starting to burst open and the dogwood blossoms still a couple of weeks away. The leaves of the maples and oaks are that iridescent young green so filled with light. Then they come upon a couple of white pines that lead to a pine grove.

Standing in the center, the trees in a kind of magical semi-circle, their bottom branches reaching out touching each other, Lydia says, "Oh, I used to love to come here. Didn't you Dan?"

Daniel turns around slowly, looking intently at each tree, as if they were old friends he was encountering after many years. He studies their wide trunks, places his hand upon one, feeling its grooves. He breathes in deeply of the clean piney sap smell and looks upward to the dark green summit. The tops of the trees almost meet, leaning in a bit, as if to form this green chapel in the woods for him, the wide-reaching branches below feeling like arms embracing him. He keeps gazing up there.

After what seems like a long time to Lydia, he kneels in the middle of the grove, turns his attention to the ground and places his hands upon it, rubbing the brittle brown needles between his fingers. Soon he sits down, crosses his legs and, with his elbows upon his knees, presses his hands together, as if in prayer.

As quietly as she can, Lydia settles herself next to him, perceiving this may be a big moment not to be lost.

"This was Evan's special place, his hideaway he took me to once in a while when we were kids. That tree was Evan's favorite."

Daniel looks up to the towering pine that seems like the elder in the circle, the one the others would consult for good counsel, if there was such a thing with trees.

"He wouldn't let me climb it, said it was too dangerous for me. And with the others, he'd be right behind me, making sure I wouldn't fall. He was always trying to protect me."

Dan bends his head toward the ground, rubs the brown needles between his fingers again, harder this time. He wants to say something, his lips moving slightly trying to find the words. He peers wide-eyed around at the trees, as if someone were going to leap out from behind them all of a sudden. He then looks up again, smiling a little manically, Lydia thinks.

"Boy, did we love it up there at the top. It was quite a feat to get there, so when we did we were pretty proud of ourselves. Then we'd be really quiet and listen to the wind through the branches. There was always wind up there, even on a summery day. If it was blustery, Evan, who pretended he was Robin Hood in Sherwood Forest when we were here, would say that was a sign the Sheriff of Nottingham and his silver armored men on black horses were coming, but not to worry because he, Evan, would protect us. I remember I felt this strange combination of being scared but brave at the same time.

"Then, if it was a soft wind, he'd say that was a good omen

and we would be rewarded. When I'd ask what that reward might be, he said we'd know it when it happened. We always felt something amazing up there, seeing out and so far above everything else, like we were more than human in some way, like we were woodland superheroes or gods of some kind."

Dan keeps staring up there. Lydia could see tears forming in his eyes.

"I never said this before to anyone. You know, when I was visiting him at college in Colorado that spring and he dove into the river and didn't come back, he was still trying to protect me. He was saving my friend Henry who fell overboard when we were white-water rafting; Evan managed to push Henry above water before a big current came and swept Evan away."

Dan lowers his eyes and looks more directly into Lydia's eyes than she can ever remember. "And then, as you know, we never talked about his death as a family. Nobody talked about it at all. Evan had drowned and that was that. Nobody ever said it happened when he was saving my friend's life. So, I felt since no one talked about it, there was a lot of shame about it, and it was mine; that I caused my brother to die because of my inability to rise to the moment, to do what I should have done. And it was all compounded because our family was so broken then. Dad was married to Laura at the time who didn't appreciate who Evan was or anything about our family, really. And Mother was such a mess. You know how she mourned Evan, and really is still mourning him after all these years, so I felt even guiltier."

Daniel buries his face in his hands and now lets the tears flow. Lydia has the strongest urge to put her arms around him, but she holds back, knowing he needs to cry some more, to allow himself to fully feel his sorrow. This might be the first time he ever faced this sadness, likely the deepest of his life.

After a while, though both have no idea how long because time has evaporated, Daniel rubs his eyes with the heels of his big hands and says, "Sorry. I never cry."

"Don't be sorry. You need to truly mourn what happened after all these years, so many years these feelings bound up inside you. I think everything will be clearer to you now, Dan, everything about your life."

Reaching for his hands, Lydia holds them fervently as she looks at his face, seeing it as she never had before, maybe since he was a child: Daniel, finally letting his guard down, his unburdened self now shining through years of dark thoughts.

The Meadow of Dreams

Lydia and Daniel start walking back along the path from the pine grove. A branch of the path leads off up a hill.

"The meadow I loved was here, just over the hill," Lydia says. "Let's go see."

With each step forward and upward, her anticipation mounts. She pictures the meadow from her dream: the tall honey-colored grass stretching as far as she could see, inviting and all-encompassing. But when they reach the top, she and Daniel gaze out at a vast housing track, one house after another the same size and shape with only slight variations in color. Scrawny little trees with a few leaves dangling from them dot patches of unnaturally green lawns.

Daniel turns to Lydia whose face seems to have faded a few shades paler. He wants to say something to help her feel better but doesn't know what, except maybe "You shouldn't be too surprised." Not very comforting, though. Just the sort of snarky comment that typically comes out of me, he thinks, in moments that ask for something more thoughtful.

"Pretty awful. But I don't think this is where it was, Lydia. I remember I used to walk through the meadow to get to my friend Arthur's house sometimes, and it might have been over there, past the houses, where it appears more open."

Lydia looks to the right where Daniel is pointing. "Yes, I think that's true," she says with a hopeful tone.

They turn back along the path, so as not to have to view the houses, and then continue east zigzagging through the trees, for there's no longer a clear trail. They begin to ascend the hill again. When they reach the crest, they come upon a children's baseball field, only a small remnant of the meadow behind the home plate fence.

Lydia, with Daniel following close behind, walks over to it. She sighs deeply, half out of sadness but out of gratefulness, too: that there is just enough tall grass to take a few steps through, to stretch out her hands and feel its silken texture, to breathe in its enlivening early spring scent. Closing her eyes, she lifts her face to the sky and spins around once.

As they walk back along the path to the parking lot, neither feels the need for words. Before opening the car door, Daniel says, "Thank you, Lydia, for convincing me to come here. I know it was really good for me, in ways that will probably take some time to completely understand. But I already feel somehow different, and maybe will even more than I can now imagine."

Ralph Redux

Lydia leans back in the comfortable chair at her desk. She smiles at the computer screen as she watches a video of a ballet dancer she's just interviewed for *Dance Today*. She cannot believe her good fortune. Just after Ralph suggested she look for a new job with a dance magazine, a position opened up for a writer/editor. And the office is even uptown, closer to her apartment than the architectural magazine office was.

The dancer in the video is performing a series of pirouettes with such speed and mesmerizing grace, eyes always returning to a certain spot forward so quickly that the viewer doesn't notice the trick, as if someone were holding an invisible string from the top of her head and spinning her around. Pure magic.

As she leaves work for her dance class, she tries to keep that image in her mind. They've been practicing pirouettes in class, and since she's been talking to and watching the best dancers in New York and from around the world, she feels, and her instructor has also said as much, her own dancing has become much more competent.

She's almost at the studio entrance when her cell phone rings. "Hey, Lydia. This is Ralph. I hope you remember me."

"Hi, Ralph. Of course, I remember you. I've been thinking

about you and wondering how you're making out at school. Guess what? I have a new job, at a dance magazine. Thanks to you, I looked into it and it just happened to work out."

"That's fantastic. Congratulations. I'm doing fine. Being back in academia has actually been easier than I thought it would be. You know, the discipline to study and all. But I guess because I had been wanting it to happen for so long, I was ready. Hey, I know it's short notice, but are you free for dinner tonight?"

"Well, I'm about to start my dance class, but it's over at seven-thirty, so we could meet at eight somewhere."

"Great. How about that same little bistro on Broadway we went to before?"

"Okay. See you there."

She's usually so focused during class that she doesn't think about anything but the steps she's trying to perform. But Lydia can't help think about seeing Ralph. It's been at least a month since she's seen him, and she'd just about given up that he'd ever call again.

Ralph is sitting at the same corner table they sat at before when Lydia arrives. His hair is a little shaggier and he's dressed more casually, in jeans and a blue sweater, than was his custom at the magazine. His eyes shine brightly from across the room. As she approaches, he rises and hugs her gently.

"Lydia, how wonderful to see you again."

Over dinner, she tells him about the magazine and the dancers she's meeting; how she's finally feeling good about her work. She tells him about her trip back to her family home and finding a little patch of meadow remaining, a magical meadow where she first learned to love dancing. And that it didn't matter it wasn't there so much in physical reality because it was alive in her heart. Lydia feels good that she can tell him things like this and he won't think she's strange. She holds back from telling him about her brother, though. Maybe another time, if there is one.

"I'm so glad you could tell me this story, Lydia. I remember your saying, when I saw you last, that during Christmas vacation you connected with something in your past that had to do with dance. So, you went back to see where it began. That's probably something we should all do: to try to connect with places in our past that haunt us, because as children we have these intense experiences associated with a particular place but not a way to completely understand them."

"Yes, I think that's right, Ralph. In the case of our family, things happened to disrupt that idyllic childhood, when we were suddenly uprooted to another place entirely, with only part of the family intact. So, there was no continuity of place. Actually, maybe there was even an intentional effort to try to *forget* that place, to lock it safely away in a remote corner of my mind. I had really forgotten how I loved to dance, it only occasionally appearing in the fogginess of a dream. It's amazing, how one remembered childhood experience of a certain place can change the course of one's life."

That night, lying in bed trying to go to sleep but not trying very hard because she's enjoying her reverie, Lydia keeps seeing Ralph's eyes, how they lit up as she spoke to him, a sign that revealed not only was he really listening but that what she said was enlivening. She closes her eyes and revives the feeling as they walked along the unusually quiet street toward her apartment; that curious feeling that traveled through her when he found her hand—as though it were the most natural thing to do—holding it in a way that felt both quickening-pulse romantic and also that he could be her best friend.

Daniel

Daniel walks down the street, the same leafy Savannah street he has walked down for many years now, leaving his office at the investment firm he's worked for a dozen years or so, passing the same quaint, mostly colonial storefronts he always has, and noticing some of the same people either going from work or into shops at this time of day. But something feels different. He looks directly at a man walking by him and smiles, just a little. He usually gazes straight ahead, not at anyone. And there's never a smile unless it's someone he knows.

He takes a left at the next street heading for Deidre's house to pick up Cole for the weekend. It's such a lovely early spring day, not too warm yet and the magnolias are in the magnificence of full bloom. He stops and stands underneath one, taking in its bold contrast of color, the pale pink part like a baby's cheek, he thinks, and the other nearly purple part like that of a fresh bruise. The scent is so heady he feels about to swoon.

Daniel arrives at the door and hesitates to knock, but not with the usual dread mixed with excitement: dread at having to see Deidre and excitement at seeing Cole. He doesn't feel the dread part at all.

The door opens. He normally will look a little off center, not into her eyes. But today he looks directly into her hazel gaze, one he felt he could never read, so enigmatic, often capricious. Her blondish curly hair rings her head like a crown, late afternoon sunlight making it almost sparkle.

"Hi, Deidre."

"Hello, Dan. Cole is almost ready." She turns around. "Cole. Your dad is here."

She looks at him more intently than usual. "You look well. Everything good with you?"

"Yes. Very good. Just got back from a little trip up north to see Lydia. We went back to our old home. It was …" He searches for the right words, looking off to her side, "quite something," he settles on.

She searches his face. "Yes, I can see it must have been."

"I…I think I came to understand some things, things from a long time ago. We took a walk in the woods behind the house." He looks down at his feet, wondering whether to continue, here on her doorstep, telling her everything he thinks he understands now that he didn't before. But before he could make such a momentous decision, she comes to his rescue.

"That sounds great, Dan. I'm really glad for you. Maybe some time you'd like to tell me about it."

She actually sounds sincere, Daniel thinks. "Well, yes. I would like to tell you about it. Maybe we could do something, I don't know—go for a walk or something like that?"

There's a moment's hesitation. Then, weighing each word, what they mean, what they *might* mean, she says, "All right. When you come back on Sunday."

After arriving at his house on the outskirts of the city, Daniel decides to do one of his and Cole's favorite things: ride their bikes in the park along the river. There's about a half-hour left before sunset, which is great to see from the riverbank. Riding behind him, Daniel sees, even in the two weeks since he's been with him, how his son's ten-year-old legs push on the peddles with easier power. Maybe it's wishful thinking, he reflects as he watches Cole's back sway slightly from side to side with each determined peddle, but he feels their bond getting closer. Maybe it's also something that, for the first time in so many years, he feels is even a possibility.

Daniel catches up. "Hey, how 'bout we stop up ahead by the big oak tree. Sunset is about to begin any moment."

"Okay, Dad."

They park their bikes, and instead of sitting on the bench in front of the tree, they sit on the ground underneath it, leaning against the trunk. Daniel looks up to the lofty crown and then remembers his grandmother's soliloquy under the live oak in Southport a few months before.

He recalls the exact words, "Thank you God for all these people here I love and for whom my fervent wish is that you can help them realize whatever they need to." And she thanked God for the tree that helped her understand something she needed to, so that she could leave this world having come to terms with some important truths. Then there was Mother and the river, my sister and her meadow, Aunt Gina and the ocean, and then, and then...me, Daniel thinks, continuing to stare up at the crown: me when I was in the pine grove with Lydia, looking up to the tops of those trees and remembering Evan. Just as my sister had anticipated, there would be a continuous thread from our grandmother to me.

"Do you see something up there, Dad?" Cole asks.

"Oh, sorry, Cole. I was just thinking about something—a grove of pine trees I re-visited when I was back at my childhood home recently on a trip with your Aunt Lydia. When I was your age, I used to love to climb them with my brother."

Cole looks from the treetop to his father's face, his head tilted questioningly. "You never talk much about your brother. I sometimes forget you even had one," he says very slowly, as if not sure whether he should be saying this at all.

Struck by the sudden truth of this, Daniel at first doesn't know how to respond. He stares at Cole for a moment, then says, "There's always been a lot of sadness about my memories of Evan. I wasn't able to talk about any of the good and happy things I guess, because of the sad things. I finally realized, going back to our family home, some important truths about Evan's life, and mine, and I feel much better now, about him and I guess about me, too. I had felt guilty about some stuff I shouldn't have."

Daniel wonders whether he should go on, tell his son more. Is ten years old too young for these conversations, about death, about guilty feelings? *I definitely need to say something about guilty feelings because otherwise he would be left with a lot of potential dark stuff to ponder about me. And isn't that exactly the problem we had in my first family—not ever talking about sad things?*

"You see, Cole, Evan was very brave and had a heroic quality about him, especially when it came to protecting me. For instance, he wouldn't let me climb the tallest trees—and I really wanted to, believe me—because I wasn't big enough. Years later, when we were both in college and I was visiting Evan in Colorado with a friend and we were white-water rafting on the river, my friend fell overboard. Evan jumped in to save him, which he did, but then suddenly a current pulled Evan away and we never saw him again.

"I always felt guilty because I thought I should have been the one to jump in after my friend. And then we never talked about Evan's death in the family. It was something no one ever brought up. So, that made me feel even worse, like everyone else thought it was my fault, too. It's important that family members talk about their feelings, I've come to realize, Cole, and especially sad stuff because that's what's hardly ever talked about and, as a result, stays caged up inside. I guess sort of like livings things, they want to be set free."

Daniel looks out at the sunset just at the moment the sun is starting to sink down, and then back at Cole who is gazing intently at his father, perhaps more intently than he ever has.

"So, if there's anything you ever want to talk about son, something that might be bothering you, I think I'll be better at listening from now on."

Biting his lower lip, wondering if he really should raise this largest of all questions, the thing that he thinks about more than anything else, Cole decides there might not be another moment quite like this.

"Well, okay then. First, thanks for telling me about your brother. I'm really glad for you, and for me, too, you can talk about him now. He sounds like he was amazing. So, the thing I'd like to ask is, I've always wondered if you and Mom might get back together. She's gone out with some guys but never more than once or twice, I think. So, maybe she still really likes you."

Daniel looks off again at the setting sun, about half-way down now, the pinks changing into orange along the horizon line. Cole is looking at it, too. Daniel puts his arm around his son's shoulder.

"Thanks for saying what you did about Evan. He truly was amazing. As far as your mom and me, I'd like us to be together again, I can tell you that much. We'll see what the future holds."

Cole Dreaming

Cole is lying in bed, about to close his eyes and fall fast asleep; the bedroom is dark except for a bright path of moonlight through the window. A tree just beyond the window is backlit from the light. It could be a magnolia, but Cole isn't sure.

He thinks of the great pine trees his father described climbing with his brother, imagines himself climbing such trees. It feels a little lonely, climbing all by himself. Would be really nice to have someone out there with me, he thinks. Not that I would be afraid at all, just that it would be more fun with someone, maybe with my best friend Lawrence.

But, as he closes his eyes, he sees someone else with him up in those tall branches. The boy deftly hooks onto a branch then follows up with his feet firmly planted on the trunk, always his eyes looking up to where he wants to go, though also looking often over to Cole, to see if he's doing okay as he makes his way up, too. Suddenly, Cole loses his grip. He starts falling down, down, so fast and he's so strangely weightless, as if he had no body at all. Like some kind of magical being out of the blue, his climbing buddy swoops down and catches him just at the last moment before he crashes to the ground.

Cole awakens—it's such a powerful sensation, that sense of falling. He almost woke up before he was caught. It all felt so very real; his heart is still racing and he's breathing very fast. His eyes wide open now, he wonders who that magical being could have been.

Daniel and Deidre

It's late Sunday afternoon as Daniel drives Cole back home. All of the weekends with his son are memorable, but this one will be especially so, Daniel reflects: those moments under the oak tree by the river, sharing thoughts they had never before shared, or even begun to share. Amazing how great it felt—and really not as hard and scary as he had always thought it might be, talking about Evan, particularly to Cole. It felt sort of like he had finally climbed to the top of that tallest pine tree and now could see out very far.

They're about to pull up to the house.

"Dad, can I tell you something?"

"Of course. Tell away."

"Well, I had this powerful dream last night. I don't usually have such dreams. I mean, I have dreams. Lots about going someplace a little strange on my bike, like a neighborhood I've never been to, where there's a super snarly barking dog tied up in a yard, but looking like he could break away at any minute. But I never have dreams like this one. I was climbing a tree with someone, and then I fell but he suddenly was able to fly and caught me before I fell to the ground. I don't know who he was. Maybe he was an imaginary brother.

"So, it got me wondering if I might ever have a brother for real. It must have been great having a brother. Even though he's not here anymore, you did have a brother for a bunch of years."

Daniel parks in front of the house and turns off the car. He stares ahead for a few moments, his eyes widening as if he's again seeing from that tallest pine tree that Evan climbed. He turns to his son sitting next to him; Cole is searching his dad's face tentatively, not sure whether he really might have gone too far this time.

"I..I never thought of Evan that way. I mean, just being grateful that I had a brother for the time I did." He shakes his head. "It's amazing. How did that song go—*'Teach your parents well....'*" He leans over and puts his arm around his son.

"You helped me to see so much. And, well, if it means anything, I'd like you to have a brother someday, too. We'll see what happens."

They get out of the car and as they approach the front door, Deidre opens it.

"Hi guys. Have a good weekend?"

"Yeah, it was good," Cole says as he looks at his dad and smiles.

Deidre gives him a hug. "That's great. Your dad and I said we'd take a walk together when you came back, so why don't you go inside and we'll be back soon, okay?"

"Sure." He smiles from one to the other. "Take your time. I'll be fine."

They walk a short way down the street and come to a neighborhood park with a bench under a magnolia tree.

"Want to sit here and have a chat? You said you'd like to tell me about your trip up north to your old home."

"Yes, I'd like to tell you some things about that, and other things since then too, maybe."

There's enough room on the bench so they're not sitting too closely, and can turn slightly toward each other. Daniel picks up a petal on the bench that had fallen from the magnolia tree. He studies it, and is reminded of how a few days ago he had thought of the flower's contrast in colors, and now it's been presented, almost magically it seems, as a perfect metaphor for the story he wants to tell. How much easier it might be to tell the story this way, too, he thinks; maybe I won't be so nervous, searching for the right words. Holding his opened palm with the petal close to Deidre's face, he begins.

"See, Deidre, how the purplish red in the petal fades to pale pink. It makes me think of a bruise, a bruise of hurt and pain becoming something new in the pale pink, something that looks fresh and innocent, like a child. Of course, one can also see it the other way around, the innocence becoming the dark of pain."

Daniel can't believe he's speaking this way; a new vocabulary and way of expressing himself seems to have blossomed.

"I figured out that I'd buried an old hurt from my childhood, a guilt I've kept all these years, about the death of my brother, Evan. I never really saw it before, until I walked into a pine grove back home where he and I used to go. I remembered how he protected me when we climbed those trees, and then how he protected me the day he drowned when he dove into the water to save my friend who had fallen overboard, so that I wouldn't dive in. Our family never talked about what happened, so I felt even guiltier about it, like somehow I was to blame.

"Now that it's come to the surface for me, I see how it's been like a bruise that wouldn't heal and that kept me unable to connect with part of myself, my feelings. And I think it had a lot to do with us, Deidre. When we had a disagreement, often I wasn't able to discuss whatever it was about, and would just walk away angry, not knowing why I was angry and not wanting to find out either.

"So, by going back to that little boy I was, I discovered the bruise, and saw that I really was not guilty after all."

Daniel briefly glances up at Diedre's eyes, then away, into the distance. He wants to keep the momentum going, to finish what he has to say, without starting to think about how she might be reacting.

"Another important thing that's happened." He shakes his head and smiles. "You know, it just amazes me how smart and aware kids can be—well, Cole anyway. So, Cole actually has helped me to see that I can think about my brother and appreciate him for the time he was on this earth. There was always just so much sorrow and hurt, I couldn't do that. It makes a big difference. To finally think about Evan and smile a little rather than wince in pain feels like a big step."

He looks directly into Deidre's eyes now. Does she think I sound like a mushy, blathering fool, he wonders? It's always so confoundingly hard to read her sylvan green eyes, so full of life but the emotional content almost impossible to discern, he thinks; sometimes she'd look at me and I'd believe she was angry at something I said or did, but then it would turn out she wasn't at all. Something about that color green, maybe, always flashing life, life, life!—however it manifests.

Then, ever so slowly, she moves her hand toward Daniel's palm with the wilting magnolia petal and places her palm over his as a mist forms over the green depths of her eyes.

Gentian

As the plane starts to descend from above the clouds, George gazes out the window, eagerly anticipating the first sign of the snow-covered peaks. How amazing to see them from above, he thinks! And how long it's been since he visited last, and then it was only to Geneva for a quick business trip. They'll be landing in Zurich, and after a short drive to Lucerne, they'll hike around the lake and up the alpine trails he hiked in his youth, something he's never done as an adult.

He glances next to him at Lydia and Daniel. He's excited but at the same time nervous. He tells himself not to look too far ahead, just enjoy every moment as it comes along, whatever that moment may bring.

"Oh, my word, Dad! I thought we had beautiful wildflowers in the states, like the ones we would find in the woods and meadows behind the house on Long Island. But never, ever anything like this," Lydia exclaims as they walk along the Swiss Path around Lake Lucerne and look out upon the panorama of flowers just beginning to bloom in the fields.

"It's only April, so I can just imagine what it will be like in the summer."

"Yes, Lyddie. Around July, as I remember, the edelweiss starts to appear. It's such a lovely little flower. We used to say they were fallen stars, because of their shape and so bright white."

The three walk off the trail into a meadow filled with purple and white crocuses, yellow primrose, white narcissus, and a small blue flower. "Do you know the name of the blue flower, Dad?" Lydia asks.

"My sister is the one who knew the names of all the wildflowers."

Lydia and Daniel glance at their father. So rarely did he ever mention his sister, from the time they were children. They hesitate to pursue this thread about her, but then Lydia senses it might be a good time. She bends down and picks one of the blue flowers.

"I know you're not supposed to pick them but maybe just one would be okay." She holds it in the palm of her hand. "Wow. What a color blue. It's almost turquoise, really." She carefully places it in her father's hand.

George stares at it for a few moments. "This is called spring gentian. It was my sister's favorite flower; in fact, she was named after it. Her eyes were this color, very beautiful, and with her red hair, people would find themselves staring at her."

He closes his fingers over it, then looks up toward the snowcapped mountains in the distance.

"We much enjoyed walking through these meadows and up the mountainsides in the spring and summer, and skiing in the winter. Gentian and I were really best friends. She was only a year younger than me. Our parents were separated, I think you know. My Dad and mother had moved to New York, where we were born, but my mother was not happy and wanted to move back to Switzerland when we were about six and seven. So, we went with her to go to school here. Father would come to visit once a year, or we would go to New York.

"I then moved back to New York after graduating from the University of Bern, and Gentian stayed here. She married a German, who became a member of the Nazi party, as almost all Germans did at the time. It was very strange to be thinking about the remote possibility of coming across him in a battle during the war. I didn't see her, of course, for a number of years, and then I heard she had died on Christmas Eve, 1944, not long before the war ended. My mother wrote to me and told me. She was only twenty-five. Apparently she had a blood disease, probably leukemia. It always has been hard to think about her for lots of reasons."

George, not usually one to feel comfortable in a natural setting, sits down in the meadow, as Lydia and Daniel do, too, forming a little circle. He opens his palm and looks at the flower.

"We were so close, you see. When our parents separated, we had each other. No one else would understand what we felt. Not many children had divorced or separated parents back then. So, it was very hard when she and I parted ways, her staying here and me going to the states.

"Then, it was difficult to accept she had married a German. But, perhaps he was a nice person—I couldn't imagine her marrying someone who wasn't—who just had to go along with things to survive. So, thinking about her brings up so many bad memories of the war, too: how unspeakably horrible it was, the death and chaos; the belief you were fighting for the very survival of freedom; and then the shock of what that meant—the killing of young men who were maybe not that different than you; but then you'd see your friends dying all around you and you'd be filled with rage and revenge. It took me a long time to recover from the worst effects. For at least a year after I came back, I had terrible nightmares and would break out in sweats. It's very hard to talk about, even now after all these years."

He bends his head forward and a tear falls from his eye onto the blue flower. Daniel and Lydia, on either side of him, place a hand on his shoulder.

After a moment, he looks up to the mountains ahead. "It is good to be back here. I feel I'm recapturing the good parts of my memory of her, and of my childhood. How we adored running through these very fields and along the mountainsides and skiing down them in the winter. How we felt protected somehow, maybe even a kind of love, surrounded by these mountains."

Lydia and Daniel look up at the mountains now; they can easily imagine that feeling of protection; it's not a stretch to imagine a feeling of love, either.

"Thank you for telling us this, Dad," Lydia says. "We're so grateful to know this history. We now know something more about you, and a lot more about Gentian. Let's save this blue flower. You can have it pressed and perhaps make a little altar with it, so you have it always to remember her, her beauty, what she meant to you, what this alpine field and these mountains meant to you.

"It's good to reclaim your buried past, Dad, as Daniel and I have, and as Nans, Mom and Gina did, too. This is the way we honor those and that which we have lost, and the way we honor ourselves, too."

"Yes, I do feel a heaviness has lifted from me." He breathes deeply. "These mountains," then he looks down at the flower, "and this little blue flower did that heavy lifting."

Springtime in Manhattan

Lydia is about to turn off her computer at work when her cell phone rings.

"Hi, Lydia. This is Ralph. How was your trip to Switzerland?"

"Oh, hello, Ralph. It was just great. I hadn't been on a trip with my dad for many years. It was…a trip of a lifetime. I guess sounds terribly cliché, but it really was, in so many ways. So, how are you? It's good to hear your voice."

"Oh, fine. Finishing up the spring semester next week. I've also got an internship starting at a firm this summer. They offered me a job once I finish up my degree at the end of the fall semester."

"That's fantastic. Congratulations. Well, I've got to go off to my dance class. Next week we're holding class outside, which I'm really excited about. We've been working on a little dance piece, to Vivaldi's "The Four Seasons," the spring and summer movements. My teacher performed the four movements with the New York City Ballet a number of years ago and has created a pared-down choreography for our dance group. It's quite beautiful, and is going to be such fun to be doing it outside, at the tail end of spring now and about a month from the beginning of summer."

"That sounds great. Where will you be doing it?"

"In Fort Tryon Park, one of my favorite places in the city."

"One of my favorites, too. On Sundays, sometimes I wander around the Cloisters listening to the Gregorian chants and then go for a walk. You can really lose yourself in that park. There's a sense of wildness there."

"Yes, I agree. I go often on Sundays, too. Funny we haven't run into each other, but it is a big place. Maybe we'll go together sometime."

"Yes. For sure. In the meantime, would you mind if I came to see your class next week, and then maybe we could go out to that little café in the park afterward?"

"Are you sure you want to see a bunch of amateurs, though some of us in the class are really good. I think I'd feel a little self-conscious with someone watching me."

"You shouldn't. After all, it is just a class."

"Yes, that's true. Well, it will be over by the Heather Garden, which will be lovely now with spring flowers in bloom. The class starts at five-thirty, and we'll be practicing a bit, getting ourselves situated, so maybe if you come around six that will be good. The two movements last about forty minutes."

"Wonderful. Looking forward to seeing you."

Lydia starts to run the water in the bathtub. The classes have been so vigorous lately, she's been taking a hot bath after each one. She pours in a capful of valerian and breathes in the vapors. Lying in the steaming water, she closes her eyes and goes over the choreography in her mind.

Her body and mind so completely relaxed after her bath, she tucks herself into bed. Drifting off quickly, halfway to sleep, she sees herself dancing in the meadow of her youth. On the edge of the meadow someone approaches. She's startled at first—she has never seen anyone in this meadow before. It appears to be...Ralph.

Saxon Woods

After parking the car, George eagerly makes his way to the preserve entrance. He's lived here in the township of Scarsdale now for twenty years; when his second marriage ended on Long Island, he returned to this city of his early childhood. But this is the first time he's visiting Saxon Woods as an adult, once a favorite place he and his sister used to come with his parents.

He hadn't wanted to visit it, until now. After his journey to Switzerland a couple of weeks ago, he realized that being in the woods always made him feel melancholy. This is why he never wanted to take walks with Eugenia behind the house on Long Island, and why he was anxious to get out of that woodland in Southport he walked in with Lydia. The woods reminded him of something he didn't want to be reminded of: his sister, rather the loss of her. Now, so much has changed.

As he hikes along the path, he looks off to the side at a giant rock outcropping, nearly fifteen feet tall and twice that around. Tall hardwood trees, now leafing out in the iridescent new green of springtime, loom in-between the rocks. George smiles, and thinks how … he looks for the words … uplifting and comforting it all is. So many years I've missed all of this.

But now I'm going to make up for it, he thinks. He places his hand on the rock and runs his hand along the smooth surface.

In the distance, he can hear water. Soon he comes upon the river, running swiftly in the springtime as it will. "The Mamaroneck River," he says out loud, enjoying the sound of the name. He bends down and feels the water with his fingers: always moving, never staying in one place, he thinks; the way we should be in our minds, not get stuck in one place. Why can't we be more like a river?

He finds a patch of lichen nearby and carefully picks a small piece. He remembers that when he and Gentian walked here with their mother, his sister would weave some lichen in her hair, like a crown, and then laugh and dance in a circle; Mother would clap and say she looked just like a forest nymph of Swiss Celtic myth.

Once back home, George retrieves the lichen from his pants pocket and places it on the mantel around a photograph he had found of his sister as a very young girl, the sepia-toned photo not revealing the color of her hair nor her eyes. Next to it was the flower from Switzerland he had pressed and enclosed in glass. It still looked almost as blue as it did when Lydia picked it.

He imagined his sister with the lichen in her red hair and the blue of her eyes shining like the flower. A little altar to Gentian, right in the middle of the living room where he can see it and contemplate it whenever he's standing there or sitting in his favorite chair. He lights the candles on either side and says, "My beautiful sister Gentian, I'm happy to have found you again."

Fort Tryon Park

Lydia strolls along the path to Heather Garden. The dogwoods and crabapples are in bloom; interspersed amongst the majestic elms, they create a magical deep pink and white understory. White and purple iris and foxglove abound in the lower vistas.

She comes to a circular setting of slate ringed with beds of columbine and red, pink and white tulips mixed with magenta and white rhododendrons. A marble fountain sits in the center of the closest circle and along the farthest ring, shaggy goats beard lends the garden a wilder look. She's glad she's arrived early before her dance classmates, to take in the gardens by herself. The exuberant color and the variety of shapes create just the right background for the dance they'll perform, she thinks.

Although a very different place than her wild meadow of memory she danced in as a girl, she remembers passing blooming dogwoods and rhododendrons in the woods on her way to the meadow in the spring. How satisfying when humans can work with nature and create something so aesthetically pleasing—like ballet itself, Lydia reflects. Many of the steps seem so unnatural; after all, what can be more unnatural than standing on point? Yet, in the gracefulness, spontaneity and illusion of effortlessness a good ballet dancer can achieve, we can see an exquisite expression of nature, of human nature, can't we? And if we properly understood ourselves, she ponders further, we would see ourselves as an ultimate expression of nature itself, a crowning glory of the poetic evolution of life on this earth; and thus, responsible to the rest of creation to care for and love it. For this we need humility.

Humility—that word! Now Lydia recalls the conversation at Christmas, when its meaning came up at the dinner table: humus, meaning earth, a returning to the earth, a remembering of what is at the base and the beginning of everything, to what is common ground. She smiles at this great circle of thought, from now to back then, before she had rediscovered dance but had intuited what connecting to nature—her own and that which is out in the world—might actually mean for her.

Suddenly, she's aware others have arrived.

"All right everyone," Nadia Beech announces in her authoritative tone as she claps her hands twice. "There's a potting shed over to the right here where we've been given permission to put our things. I hope you have all worn some of the colors I suggested—white for the women and blue for the men.

"It's going to be such a delight dancing here, don't you think? Dancing this lovely spring and summer ballet outside, where it belongs. This circular area is just the right amount of space. I came here before, of course, to make sure the surface would be smooth and even enough. We will enter from the right here and exit to the left. I will put the CD player by the fountain there. Now, come, let us pretend we have an admiring audience and begin our fun little performance!"

Lydia remembers Ralph is coming; she won't have to

pretend there's an admiring audience. Nervous thoughts start to tense her fingers and toes: she'll forget the difference between a battement and a grand jete' and when she should be doing each. Oh, why did I ever think I could start over doing this at thirty-eight years old, she thinks?

As they begin, the lead dancers looking so poised and confident, Lydia's worries begins to wane. And then, as she enters and begins her pirouettes, arabesques and sautés, she leaves behind all other thoughts and simply delights in her body moving in time and space—this inspiring space amidst the trees, flowers, and the flowing fountain water with Vivaldi's music thrillingly capturing spring and summer: the quivering violins sounding like the stirring of new life from nests, buds, and under the earth; and in the summer movement, the rousing allegros feeling like life abounding, then shifting dramatically to languorous adagios that hint of a sultry summer day.

Lydia is carried away with it all and doesn't notice Ralph who's trying to be inconspicuous screened behind the goats beard on the farthest edge. A few others, walking through, stop to look.

When the performance is over, all the dancers applaud Nadia and thank her for giving them the chance to dance this beautiful ballet outside. The two lead dancers say they hope Nadia will choreograph the other two movements they can perform outside in early October, when it's still warm enough and the trees will be glorious in their autumnal colors.

Putting on her skirt and sweater over her tights and changing from ballet shoes to walking shoes, Lydia emerges from the shed and sees Ralph by the fountain. He walks toward her, smiling, and puts his arms around her.

"Lydia, I so enjoyed that. I've never been to an outdoor dance performance, and in this setting, it was enchanting.

Not that I'm any kind of expert in dance, but everyone looked really good."

"Oh, I'm so glad you liked it, Ralph. Yes, I think Nadia is a quite brilliant choreographer. We are very lucky to have her as our teacher. She could have her own professional dance troupe, but I think she doesn't want all the pressure that goes with that. And some of the dancers could be professional too, I think, but aren't for the same reason."

They walk to the restaurant not far away where Ralph has reserved an outdoor table. It's a beautiful garden setting. They sit down and immediately a waiter brings out a bottle of champagne.

"I thought you might deserve a toast," Ralph says.

"Oh, how sweet of you. It was just a class, though, not a real performance."

"Yes, but I think it was more than a class for you. From what you told me, finding dance again was a very big deal. And this was your first sort of performance, right? And it was outside, reminiscent of that meadow you told me about you danced in as a young girl, am I right?"

"Yes, I suppose it is an occasion for me to celebrate. It's so thoughtful of you, Ralph—and to remember those little details I told you. Makes me feel, well, I guess that you care."

He looks intently into her eyes. "Yes, I do care—a lot." He raises his glass. "To you, Lydia. And to your future, with dance and, I hope, with me. I would like us to spend a lot more time together. I hope you want to, too."

Lydia holds up her glass. "Yes, I can think of nothing I'd like more."

The River

Daniel leans forward and pulls on the oars, never taking his eyes off the two passengers sitting in front of him. Her green eyes are fixed on him and Cole's are looking off to the side at the small wake his father's strokes are creating in the calm river. Cole sticks a few fingers into the passing water, careful not to move too suddenly and rock the boat, disturbing the tranquil moment.

Daniel relaxes his hold on the oars, letting the boat quietly drift. Looking at Cole, he sees how much his son is beginning to resemble Evan—the copper red hair, the golden brown eyes and expressive eyebrows, the wide smile and handsome shape of his face. He remembers a wonderful photo hidden in a desk draw, given to him by an old girlfriend of Evan's, that he hasn't been able to look at it for all these years. I'm going to get it out and frame it, put it on my desk, where I can see it, and Cole can, too, he thinks. Cole has never seen a picture of his uncle.

"This is so fun, Dad. You know, I can't remember us ever doing this before. Did I maybe forget?"

Daniel is a bit taken aback. Can it be true he hasn't gone boating with Cole, ever? Gone biking, hiking, skating, swimming, camping, and fishing off the riverbank, played basketball and baseball, but did they ever go out in a boat?

"I remember we all went on an afternoon riverboat cruise," Deidre says. "I think you were only about six, Cole. Do you remember it? It was here, on this river."

"Oh, yeah. I do remember that. Why didn't we ever go on a boat after that?" Then Cole suddenly thinks of Evan and his dad on the boat in the river rapids, and Evan diving into the water to save his dad's friend, never to return.

"It's okay, Dad. I think I know why."

Realizing what Cole has now understood, Deidre puts a hand on his knee, and her other hand on Daniel's knee in front of her. "Maybe we can all go on some more boat rides now."

Daniel feels like shedding a tear and smiling at the same time, filled with gratitude as he is: for the understanding of the two people he loves most in the world; for the ability to simply *feel* things as he hasn't ever before; and to experience how sadness can become gladness.

He reaches out and squeezes Deidre's hand with one hand and Cole's with his other.

The Camellia

As she looks up at the blooming red camellias in the yard, Eugenia is reminded that Christmas is not far away.

"Christmas is going to be so festive this year, Gina," she says to her great aunt sitting in her wheelchair underneath one particularly large camellia bush. "Everyone is coming. Did I tell you that Daniel and Deidre have gotten back together, so we'll have all three of them? It's going to be so wonderful to see my grandson. And did I tell you Lydia has a new boyfriend and they're both coming? She said George is coming too; she didn't want him to spend Christmas by himself. We're going to have to find some extra chairs for the dining room."

Gina lifted a gnarled hand and waved it in front of her, as if clearing away cobwebs. "Well, isn't that just swell. Yippee! A big party. I hope I'll still be around to enjoy it."

"It's only less than three weeks away, Gina. I think you'll be around," Eugenia says with a smile.

"Hah. Sometimes I think I'll be around forever! Gosh, too bad Zipporah isn't with us any longer. She sure would have enjoyed herself. She always loved a big party. The more the merrier with her, right Gigi?"

"Yes, I think that was true. She liked being the center of

attention, too. Funny, how different we were, Gina. I would shrink from a crowd, which consisted of anything more than one person, and mother would revel in it. I guess I must be more like my Dad, though I'm not sure what he was like. I always blamed mother for that. Now I'm glad all that blaming is over."

Eugenia reaches up and carefully plucks a camellia flower from the bush that's now tall enough to be a tree.

"You know, Gina, when I look at my own marriage, I can see now how I was repeating a pattern and didn't realize I was, leaving George the way I did, without enough reason really."

She stares at the flower, its deep, passionate redness, and as she affixes it behind her ear, says, "Oh, the mistakes we make! If we could get do-overs, how different our lives might be."

"Oh, isn't that the truth, Gigi darlin'. But from this far vantage point," Gina says as she waves her hand in front of her a few times, as if clearing away even more cobwebs, "I see that we do get do-overs. Of course, not the same thing over again 'cause nothing in life ever repeats itself exactly the same way. Look at Daniel and Deidre, for instance—they're getting a do-over, right? And then how 'bout you and Zipporah? You two got a sort of do-over in the end. And you and Lydia—haven't you two had a coming-together? Maybe something's in the air and even you and Georgie will get a do-over, too."

Eugenia stares at her great aunt, her eyes widening. "Oh no, how could that happen at our age?" she says incredulously. "There've been so many years," she adds, her voice trailing off. The camellia falls from behind her ear, then she picks it up.

"I've always loved this kind of camellia, the Yuletide, so perfect for this time of year with its cheerful red blooms and dark green leaves."

"You know, back in Victorian times when I was born, Gigi, the meaning of different flowers was important to folks. If I

126

remember correctly, according to the most popular notion, a camellia had something to do with love and destiny. You'd give it to someone you thought you could trust with your life and your love to the ends of the earth and the end of time."

Eugenia stares again at the flower, contemplating the meaning her great aunt revealed. "Let's go inside now Gina, and put this in some water so it can last a little longer."

Eugenia and Gina Dreaming

Eugenia dabs her brush into the red paint. Glancing again at the camellia in its dish of water, she applies a carefully considered last stroke to one of the petals she's painting. She tilts her head and studies it: is it finished or should I add a dash more red, she wonders? But she's re-learning what she had known as a little girl: that less is invariably better in watercolor because you cannot easily subtract something once it's been added.

She blows on it to make sure it's dry and carries it over to where her aunt is sitting in the living room. "Gina, what do you think?"

Gina holds it close to her face. "It looks lovely, darlin'. I think you got the reds just right. I'm so glad you're painting again. I remember when you did watercolors as a girl and Zipporah would hang them up all over the place, in the kitchen and living room. Everywhere she could."

"Funny, I didn't think she liked them, but now that you mention it, I do recall she put them up around the house. I had always thought only my father admired them. You know, when we left him, mother and me, I don't think I ever did another painting."

"It's good you've found this again, Gigi, bringing back some of that happy little girl you were. Yesterday you said you didn't ever get to know your father. Well, I want to tell you he was a very sweet, kind man with a whopping good sense of humor, one of the things I think your mother liked most about him, and devilishly handsome to boot. Oh brother! Zipporah was tickled pink to have captured him, as lots of young women had their sights set on him. He was the number one catch of the town back then."

Eugenia smiles. "Yes, I remember even as a girl how attractive he was, and imagined how easy it would have been to have a crush on him."

As she drifts off to sleep, Gigi sees herself in a small motorboat on the Cape Fear River, much like the scene in the dream she had before. But this time the handsome man in the Panama hat is in the boat with her, not standing on the side of the river waving goodbye. Also in the boat is her mother. The man is confidently steering, and the mother is looking at him admiringly, then at her daughter who is painting a watercolor of the three of them in the boat puttering serenely down the river.

Gina never knows how much she actually sleeps at night anymore. It seems to her there's not that much difference between her waking and sleeping life, as she nods off to sleep both during the day and night, and has strange visions that could be dreams but could also be awake visions. Lying in bed, she doesn't feel the same anxiety she often feels at night, thinking about Harry and Gordon, and sometimes even talking to them, too.

She feels quite calm as she doses off and finds herself on a white sandy beach, a strange beach because old oaks are growing on it. She's standing by the shore, looking out far, far across the sea. She sees a big boat along the horizon, getting larger as it comes closer. Then, suddenly, it is there right in front of her. She wades into the water and sees two men on the deck. They're waving to her. She waves back and says, "Harry and Gordon, where the devil have you two been all this time. It's bout' time you've come home."

The Wooden Soldier

Eugenia positions the stuffed happy Santa with the blue eyes and red cheeks in his customary chair in the living room, then the angels with their flowing platinum hair and candles in their hands, grown more delicate with age, on the mantel. Though she's done this for so many years, the exact same way, somehow this year feels different.

She used to place them, and all the other Christmas ornaments, in their particular spots without thinking much about them. In fact, she reflects now, maybe she had an unconscious intention *not* to think about them, as they reminded her too much of the happy Christmases of long ago with George, Daniel, Lydia, and Evan.

But this year, she looks intently, and with a smile, at each decoration, as if greeting long-lost friends.

At the bottom of the box, Eugenia sees the one she has not taken out for so many years now. She picks it up carefully, as if after all these years it could break easily. It's a Nutcracker-like wooden soldier dressed in a red uniform and a black helmet. He's holding a wooden sword upward, as if in exclamation; his eyes are bright and he's smiling. She had bought it when

Evan was about a year old, before the other children had come along. It was his favorite Christmas decoration.

Something about the soldier reminded her so much of Evan, not simply that it was his favorite. Maybe it was in the expression of confronting the world with a sense of fearlessness, but, at the same time, an irrepressible gladness. Yes, this is how she thought of Evan in everything he undertook, risky or not. And God knows he had surely undertaken some risky endeavors in his short life, from daredevil skiing to motorcycle racing.

She carefully places the toy in the middle of the dining room table. Evan was going to join them in spirit. For the first time in—she can't remember when, probably since he'd been gone—she smiled at his memory instead of shedding tears or else imagining he was actually *not* gone but just lost somewhere in the shadows and mists of the world.

Eugenia and George

Eugenia is in the kitchen beginning to make dinner. The sun is starting to set, and she looks up through the window above the sink just at the moment the sun begins to fall away—so quickly, she thinks. It disappears so fast that you really have to pay attention or else you'll miss it. How many things I missed because my mind was elsewhere, drifting, not thinking about anything important.

But lately, she thinks, I'm noticing how my mind doesn't seem to wander as much, how I'm able to focus more and not miss so much. Maybe it's because of the painting. Yes, it's helping me to see more what is in every moment. Could it also have something to do with Evan? Could being unable to think about him in an honest way all these years have accustomed my mind to avoidance, to not being able to feel truly comfortable in any given moment?

She smiles and turns on the water to fill the pot. She hears a light knock at the front door. Rarely does anyone come to visit at this time. She goes to the door and opens it.

"Why, George. What a surprise. I didn't expect you for another couple of days."

"Hello, Eugenia. Lydia told me to come on this day, so I

did. Maybe I got it wrong. I'm awfully sorry. I can find some things to do in the area for a couple of days. I'm sure there's probably a golf course somewhere nearby."

"Oh, really, it's fine. Please come in. I was just starting to make dinner for Gina and me."

"Oh, thanks. But I don't want to disturb you."

"You aren't disturbing me. Please, I insist. And Gina would, too, I'm sure."

He's completely unsure whether to accept her invitation. He always feels so awkward and nervous around Gigi because she makes such a fuss over him, probably because she feels nervous and awkward, too.

"Why don't I sit out here on the porch for a bit, if it's okay? I just arrived and the evening is nice and so much warmer than up north right now, of course. It was snowing when I left."

"Oh, yes. Can I get you a drink perhaps? If I remember, you like a dry martini with a twist of lemon. I don't think I have any gin, but I do have vodka. Would that be okay?"

"That would be fine. Actually, I have switched to vodka myself. Hard to drink gin anymore and keep my wits about me."

George decides to settle into a wicker rocking chair that looks as if it's been around for a while, the white paint flaking on the arms, but otherwise quaintly inviting and sturdy enough. Normally, he'd choose a straight-backed chair. However, he knows the rocker will help him relax after his flight to Wilmington, then drive to Southport, and now in Eugenia's midst.

He gently pushes back the rocker, trying not to think about how nervous Eugenia will make him feel when she returns. But already he's noticing she seems less frenzied in his presence than she customarily is. And, arriving unexpectedly as he did, she would be an absolute whirling dervish of nerves, he thinks to himself, yet she seems almost calm. Eugenia returns with a drink in each hand.

"I hope I made it the way you like. It's been a while since I've made a martini—my martini days were over many moons ago. I can only manage vodka and orange or cranberry juice, with the emphasis on the juice."

She sits in the wicker rocker on the other side of the small table between them. Feeling a bit anxious, she takes a sip of her drink, rocks back and forth a few times and, looking out ahead at a camellia bush, begins to be more at ease.

"I can't wait to hear all about your trip to Switzerland with Lydia and Daniel. Lydia told me a little about the beautiful place you went to, but I think she wanted to let you talk more about it. Was it a wonderful trip?"

"Oh yes, yes it was. I hadn't been to the place of my childhood since...well, since I was a child. It was different, of course, but some things were the same: the spring wildflowers in the meadows, the snow-capped mountains in the distance. Brought back many fond memories."

He hesitates to go further. He had never shared much about his childhood with Eugenia when they were married, and it seemed even stranger to share anything like that with her after all these years of being divorced. Yet, even so, something urges him on. He takes another sip from his glass.

"The meadows brought back many memories of my sister Gentian. How we loved to run through those meadows and up and down the mountainsides. It was a beautiful, sort of awe-inspiring experience way back then. We were very close, she and I, I think especially because our parents were separated. I recalled moving to the states after college, and her staying in Switzerland. When the war came, how painful it was knowing she was married to a German. Then, Gentian died on Christmas Eve in 1944, just before the war was over. It was the reason, I think you knew Gigi, that I always had such a hard time being happy on Christmas.

"But, you know, I think I've come to a point now, having gone back to that place of my childhood and let all those memories well up from inside, I feel—I don't know exactly how to say it—like a part of me that was buried became part of the living. I found an old photograph of my sister and put it on my living room mantel at home, along with a flower Lydia had picked from the meadow in Switzerland, a gentian flower, which I had pressed and enclosed in glass. It is my little memorial to her I can look at now with some happiness."

Eugenia gazes at George as if she's seeing someone she hadn't seen before. She can't remember him ever being this open and forthcoming about his past, or his present, for that matter, and especially involving anything emotional. She wants to reach out and touch his arm, his hand, to connect with him without any words because words seem superfluous at the moment. She decides that would be far too risky and settles on a few words, avoiding too much sentimentality that would surely make him recoil.

"That is such a lovely story, George. I'm more than grateful you could tell it to me, too. And I'm so glad it has led you to find some peace. Let me offer a toast—to you and to Gentian."

They clink their glasses, looking at each other in the eyes for a couple of moments, which is more than they had in a long, long time.

They rock their chairs, take sips of their drinks and gaze out at the camellia bush.

"Well, the big new thing in my life is I've started painting again. You probably never knew I painted because I hadn't since I was very young. It's been challenging and fun to try to get back those sorts of skills, not so much the painting skills themselves, but the patience to take my time trying to see something."

"That sounds great, Eugenia. I remember you were interested in art and had a good eye for paintings. What do you think inspired you to start again, if I may ask?"

"Remember when we were all together last New Year's Eve, talking about the many recent events: the boat ride sprinkling my mother's ashes, Lydia's realization about the meadow in her dream and my own dream about going down a river in a boat waving goodbye to my father?"

"Yes, I distinctly recall your talking about that dream. It was quite significant to you."

"Yes. In that dream, even though I was sad saying goodbye to my father, I became happy when I began painting the scenery and the wildlife around me. Then, Lydia suggested maybe it was a message to start painting. So, it may seem strange to do something because of a dream. But, you know, maybe it's just another way of learning.

"The other important step for me has been to understand, and put to rest, things I had held against my mother, as I said when we were on the boat to scatter her ashes." Eugenia shakes her head and smiles.

"It's funny, I even just learned from Gina that my mother actually liked my paintings and put them up around the house, though I had always imagined she hated them. I sure did get that ass-backwards, to use one of my mother's favorite expressions!" They laugh a little at this memory of Zipporah.

Eugenia hesitates to say more: It's certainly risky to delve into this area, but, she thinks, if not now, when? There can't ever be a better time than this.

"I also realized something else important: how in my resentment of my mother leaving my father the way she did,

I actually ended up, perversely, going down that same road myself. They had their arguments for sure, but what made her finally leave was she suspected him of having an affair. I remember there were lots of beautiful women around him, selling those fancy yachts to movie stars as he did. And mother was just so headstrong, she didn't want to think she might have been wrong.

"So, she just left with me in tow. She wanted me to think she was strong. And so, part of me admired that, I guess. And then, for whatever reason—how do we ever know the exact reasons we do things—I did the same thing."

Suddenly comprehending what Eugenia is saying, George opens his eyes wider in near disbelief, staring at her. After all these years, for the first time she is saying she made a mistake in leaving me? He doesn't know what to say.

"I am sorry, George, though that seems grossly inadequate. I'm sorry I let my suspicious nature overcome my reason. Even when I wavered a bit, my pride—what my mother said, too, was one of the foolish emotions that propelled her to leave her husband—got in the way. I think we might have continued to have a lovely life together, and the children would have had their parents together. But it is all in the past now, though I hope we can be better friends going forward."

She reaches out and touches his hand lightly with her fingertips.

George shifts his gaze downward, though he doesn't move his hand from her touch. After a few moments, he turns and looks at her intently.

"I know you thought I was having an affair, Eugenia, and I should have tried harder to dispel you of that notion. I think I was so flattered by all the attention I was getting, and was in such a state of mind at the time—the headiness of my business success, the money pouring in, the praise and appointments to this and that—that I was willing to sacrifice the most important things to my own sort of puffed-up pride."

Not able to look her in the eyes any longer, he turns his head away. "It took me many years to understand this, and many years of losing almost everything, even a second marriage, then slowly building my life back. But, even though I did remarry, Gigi, I will tell you now I never loved anyone the way I loved you."

He feels her fingertips upon his hand start to tremble. Years and years can tumble by, like so many dried up, fallen leaves tossing in the autumn wind, so many lonely thoughts that lingered late into the night. Can there be something that remains, in a touch of flesh?

He turns his hand over and enfolds her fingers in his. How different they feel—the skin no longer smooth—yet there's something familiar. They both look out ahead at the camellia bush, its flowers only slightly curling around the petals' edges but still deeply, darkly red.

Christmas Redux

Eugenia places the eighth set of silverware on the dining room table. There haven't been eight people for dinner here ever, she thinks. And, come to think of it, even so many years ago, when Evan was alive and the family was all together on Long Island, at the most there were six for Christmas Eve dinner, with Zipporah joining them when she lived nearby.

She hears bells ringing on the front door.

"Hi, Mom. I thought I'd ring the old sleigh bells. They make a very jolly sound."

They hug each other. "Lydia, how wonderful to see you."

"And great to see you. Mom, this is Ralph."

She extends her hand. "So nice to meet you, Ralph. And delighted you are joining us for Christmas."

"Thank you so much for having me."

"Let's go inside and you can say hi to Aunt Gina. The others should be here soon."

"Has Dad gotten here yet?"

"Yes. It seems a little bird told him to come two days ago." She gives Lydia a knowing look.

"Yes, I admit it, I hope it was okay. I just thought...."

"Yes, it was more than okay." She gives her daughter another hug.

As they go inside, Lydia exclaims, "Everything looks so lovely, Mom. All of the old Christmas decorations, all in their special spots. Aunt Gina, Merry Christmas." She bends over to hug her. Every year she sits a little lower in her favorite stuffed chair.

"And same to you, darlin'. Who's the handsome devil you got with you?"

"This is Ralph, Ralph, great Aunt Virginia. Really she's my great, great aunt, or maybe it's great grandaunt, but that's a lot of greats so I call her Aunt Gina for short."

"So nice to meet you, Aunt Gina. I've heard a lot about you from Lydia."

"Can't imagine what she might have told you. I'm really not that interesting, but I guess after ninety-nine years on this earth, there must be at least something to say about me." She giggles, like a little girl. "Zipporah, or Popo as we called her, was the interesting one. She was always the life of the party."

"Yes, I'm sorry Ralph won't get a chance to meet her. But I think she'll be here very much in spirit," Lydia says.

The sleigh bells ring, and in come Daniel, Deidre, and Cole. Hugs are exchanged all around and Lydia introduces them to Ralph.

"Why don't we all come into the dining room and, hopefully, George will be here soon," Eugenia says.

She helps Gina into her wheelchair and wheels her into the dining room. There's a knock at the door.

"I hope I'm not late," George says as Eugenia opens the door.

"No, we're just going in for dinner now. It will be such a special Christmas Eve this year, and it wouldn't be as special without you, George."

Everyone is gathering in the dining room as George enters.

"Dad, I'm so glad you could come," Lydia says. As she hugs him, she whispers in his ear, "and I hope you enjoyed your time the past couple of days." He whispers back, "Yes, it happens I did. You do think of everything, Lydia."

"You met Ralph before, Dad, when we went out to dinner in the city."

"Yes, nice to see you Ralph, and to have you here for Christmas."

"You'll see names by each place setting," Eugenia announces, "because there're individual gifts for each of you. I know we usually exchange our Christmas presents tomorrow, but I wanted you all to have yours from me tonight."

Everyone finds his or her place. At every setting is a white tissue-wrapped, thin, rectangular package.

"I hope everyone might share a few words about their gift," Eugenia says. "Maybe the most important present is the one in the middle of the table, in honor of Zipporah. She was the one who inspired us to re-discover the places you'll see represented in your gifts. Lydia, I think you should open that one, and that's where we should begin."

Lydia retrieves the package and carefully unwraps the tissue paper. It's a small watercolor painting, about nine by six inches. She turns it around so everyone can see it.

"This is the live oak tree Nans called Lovers' Oak which she stood underneath that day a year ago and made her revelatory speech. This is where she urged us to discover what we needed to in our own lives. And she thanked God for trees like this that helped her understand something important from her past.

"Oh, Mom, I see you even painted a little heart on the tree trunk, with the names Popo and Effie inside it. Popo was what some of us called Zipporah for short, and Effie was a nickname for her husband, Effingham.

"It's just so beautiful, Mom. Thank you for doing this. And congratulations on becoming such a good painter. You told me you had taken up painting after a very long time, but you certainly have made amazing progress."

"Thank you, Lydia. I've been working at it. This one I was able to paint while looking at the scene. For most of the others, you'll see, I had to use my imagination, which is quite a bit harder, for me anyway."

Lydia places the painting back in the middle of the table and unwraps her gift. It's a watercolor of a meadow of tall golden grass, a girl leaping through it, her arms and legs outstretched and face turned upward toward the sun.

"Oh, it's perfect, too, Mom. Thank you so much. It's like the meadow where I loved to go when I was a young girl and dance. I did go back there, with Daniel, as some of you know, on our trip to our old home some months ago. The meadow isn't there anymore, but that wasn't important. What was important was connecting with what it meant to me. I have started to dance again, which is wonderful for me, and I have a new job with a dance magazine that I love. My life is much brighter because of remembering this meadow."

Daniel unwraps his package. The painting is of a white pine grove in a semicircle. In the middle of the grove are two boys, the taller one pointing to the tops of the trees and the other gazing upward. Daniel turns the painting around so everyone can see it.

"It's much like the actual pine grove, Mother. Amazing. I did visit it on my trip with Lydia. It was still there, almost as I remembered it. So many memories streamed back as I sat there: of Evan and me climbing those trees, spending many hours in that deep green haven.

"It was so good for me to go back. It helped me work out lots of things, mostly having to do with Evan's death. And my life is vastly better now." He looks to his side at Deidre and Cole.

"Thank you for this, Mother, and to you, Lydia for convincing me go back there with you, and to my grandmother, who got us all started on these journeys."

George looks around the table. "I guess I'll go next." After removing the paper, he stares at it for a few moments. "This is quite remarkable, Eugenia. Did you just do this in the last couple of days?"

"I had done a painting before; something sort of generic depicting the Alps. But when you described it more to me the other day, the meadow of wildflowers in particular, I was able to better envision it and did another one."

He holds the painting so the others can see it. The mountains are in the background and a meadow of mostly blue wildflowers is in the foreground, in the midst of which stand a boy and a girl. He holds a small flower in his hand he's presenting to the girl.

"Some of you know the story now. It was life-changing, I think, to go back there and experience what I did in remembering my sister, Gentian, who died on Christmas Eve when she was twenty-five years old. Since going back, I've been able to deal with lots of memories, about the loss of my sister, and many about the war, too."

George pauses, thinking about how to say what he wants to say next. "Something more intangible has also come to my attention, something to do with re-connecting to the physical world and recapturing a kind of innocence, might be one way to say it. It seems I've lived so much in my head, in the world of achieving things to make me feel successful. Now I'm discovering the happiness to be found in not trying to achieve anything, in just being.

"There's a beautiful park where I live in in New York that Gentian and I used to enjoy. She and I lived in Scarsdale with our parents when we were very young, and then later, after our parents separated, we'd visit the park with my father. It's been enlivening to experience that place again.

"So, I thank you, Gigi, for this thoughtful gift. I'll certainly find a special place for it back home. And of course, I'm grateful to you, Lydia, for getting me to go on the trip to Switzerland to begin with, and to Zipporah for spurring all of us on."

"Well, it's been a privilege really, to be able to make these paintings for you all. I enjoyed it so much, I even made one for myself. But Gina, before I say anything about mine, you should open yours."

"Darlin', I have to say, you sure have outdone yourself with all this painting. You didn't have to do anything for me. But thank you anyway, and let's see what surprise you got for little old me."

Gina's shaky hands slowly unfold the tissue paper. When she finishes, she holds the painting close to her face so she can see it better.

"Looks like a lovely seascape. Well, I'll be darned. I see it's Oak Island Beach, with the big oak trees there. And there's a lady standing there looking out to sea. That's the beach I used to love to go to, I think I told most of you, and then I stopped going after Harry and Gordon were lost.

"But I'm able to go there now, and Gigi has taken me a number of times. I had a swell time just sitting near the beach on the walkway, looking out at the waves and feeling like I'd come home."

She turns the painting around to show everyone.

"Well, what a treasure this is, Gigi. I'll find a special spot for it in my room. And many thanks to you, Lydia, who got us goin' on these various excursions down Memory Lane. And of course, to my darlin' Popo, who started it all that day under the big old oak tree of hers."

"It was a great pleasure to paint that for you, Gina, more than I can really say. Well, it won't be a surprise to most of you that the painting I did for myself is of a little girl going down a river in a boat, painting pictures, my dad at the helm steering and my mother sitting looking at him and smiling. That's the happy ending to my journey. Thanks to my mother for her inspiration, and to my daughter I'm finally appreciating for the deeply thoughtful person she is. I hope it's not too late."

"I think I can claim to be the authority on that, darlin'. If it's not too late for me to learn things, it's probably not too late for anyone," Gina says. Everyone laughs along with Gina.

"I'm so glad to be part of this family again," Deidre says after a moment, her green eyes shining brightly. "I love all of your stories and am grateful for your sharing them. I'm of course particularly grateful for Dan's, which was what led to our reuniting. It was very kind of you, Eugenia, to make a painting for me." She turns it around. It's of a magnolia tree in bloom.

"I don't know how you could have known, but the moment Dan and I knew we were meant to be together again was while we sat underneath a magnolia tree."

"Oh, isn't that marvelous!" Gigi claps her hands and says. "It's just a pure coincidence. I painted our magnolia tree here in the yard one day recently when it was in full bloom."

Cole opens his present. "I wonder what mine is going to be." The painting is of a man, woman, and boy in a rowboat in a river.

"Wow, that's really awesome, grandma. How did you know about the boat ride?"

"Oh, your dad happened to mention something about it to me. So, I thought that sounds like a good thing to paint for you."

"Thanks so much. I hope I can learn to paint like you someday."

"Maybe I can give you a few lessons."

"That would be awesome, grandma."

After a couple of moments of quiet, Ralph says, "Well, I'm really the outsider here. I feel almost like I'm sitting in on a very private conversation."

"Oh, please don't feel that way. We're so happy to have you here with Lydia," Gigi says energetically.

"Yes, really. She's the one largely responsible for all of these stories," Daniel joins in. "And you're part of her life, so you definitely belong here, too."

"Thanks everyone. Well, let's see what the painter extraordinaire has in store for me," Ralph says as he peels away the paper from his gift. It's a scene of dogwood trees and rhododendron in bloom and a man standing amidst them peering out at a ballerina on point in the foreground.

"I know Lydia must have told you about this or else you really are clairvoyant," Ralph says as he shows everyone the painting. "Thank you, Eugenia. I'll treasure it as a pivotal event in my relationship with Lydia. Seeing her dance amidst the trees and flowers in the park convinced me of what I suspected from the beginning when we met at the magazine—that she is a rare and beautiful spirit indeed." He turns and gives Lydia a kiss on the cheek.

"Yes, it's such a great memory, Mom. I loved dancing in this park. It was the next best thing to a wild meadow. When I was there, I thought about how in a park and garden we see that people can work with nature to make something beautiful. And then I thought that in dance we see an exquisite expression of human nature, of the beauty we can create as creative beings. And if we understood ourselves correctly, we would see ourselves as the epitome of the evolution of life on earth, of its consciousness, and thus responsible to the rest of creation to care for it. For this we need humility.

"And that brought me back to remembering our conversation last Christmas, right around this table, about the meaning of that word. It comes from the Latin root humus, meaning earth, a returning to the earth, a remembering of what is at the base and beginning of everything, to what is common ground. Everyone in our family has gone on a journey back to their roots in a special place in nature, and has come back the better for it. And now, we've shared those journeys with each other, and we are the better for that as a family, I think."

"That's right, Lydia. I recall your talking about humility, and how I thought it was such a weird conversation," Daniel says, laughing at himself. "I guess I've come a ways since then. And you know, I was thinking about the word remember, how if you take it apart it means a kind of re-membering of yourself, like parts of you that were missing are found and you can become whole again by going back to your past with an openness and, I guess you could say, humility."

Everyone is quiet for a few moments, as if in a silent prayer of thanks.

"Thank you, Daniel, for that, and Lydia for your words," Eugenia says. "There's one person who has been mentioned but I think needs mentioning—remembering—again. And that is Evan.

"That little wooden soldier in the middle of the table I gave to Evan for Christmas when he was a year old. It was a favorite of his. It's the first time I've taken it out in many years.

"We were all traumatized by Evan's death, and never talked

about it together as a family, as we should have, even though we were scattered here and there. We could have made an effort. I'm sure it would have made a very big difference to all of us, particularly to Daniel and to me. I've not been able to think of him without ending up in tears, until now. And Daniel never should have felt the guilt he felt. If we had talked about what happened, then Dan probably would have been spared those feelings.

"Maybe, in some mysterious way, Evan was the one who called us back, back to remembering. He was a big-hearted, brave, and beautiful soul. Let us make a toast and give thanks to Evan for being with us on this earth for a while," Eugenia says, as she holds up her glass of wine.

All raise their glasses. "To Evan" is said in unison.

Then Lydia adds, "And to all of us."

Acknowledgments

Many voices from my familial past contributed to the inspiration to write this novel, some of whom I recognized in the dedication but others whom I didn't. North Carolina cousin Lois Jane would be one of them, among the liveliest and funniest people I've ever known. Her animated conversations with her pet parrot and her huge pots of Hoppin' John on New Year's day remain vivid in my mind. But I just couldn't fit in every ancestral voice that spoke to me. I'd like to thank my cousin, Dr. Jim I. Jones, who read a very early chapter of this novel and looked forward to my finishing it someday. My interest in my ancestors and their contribution to who I am was revived through my son Forrest's curiosity about his ancestors, and his deep pursuit of indigenous ancestral knowledge from other cultures. I'm grateful to him for this, and to my husband, Peter, for being such a patient and forgiving friend. And I'm thankful for the good writerly advice and encouragement from Jack Driscoll, and to Laurel Dodge for her careful reading.

Praise for *The Last Resort*

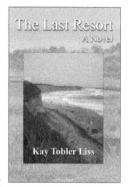

"Kay Tobler Liss's The Last Resort deals with an issue with global resonance in our times: how the needs of modern development encroaching on old ways of life drive them to a slow extinction. The Last Resort is about the conflict between the two sides involved in this narrative: the oppressors—states and corporations—and the tribal groups inhabiting ancient lands that have fallen prey to the insatiable needs of development.

Paul Collins, a city-based corporate attorney, comes to Montauk, [a town on the eastern tip of Long Island, N.Y.], to escape his decaying marriage and his professional life....[where] he meets Oshanta, who belongs to a Native American group....

Oshanta slowly opens the window of the Montauk world and its natives to Paul...[who] slowly discovers a renewed interest in life—a cause to throw himself into, a place to find refuge in, and a love to live for. Trying to prevent the land from being used for a golf course, he decides to use his lawyerly skills...to fight on the side of the beleaguered.

Kay Tobler Liss has dealt with the novel's technical aspects deftly. Written in the first person with Paul Collins as the narrator, the narrative slowly widens its scope as it progresses, taking into its sweep the complete history of the land and its people, down to its fauna and flora. (Some of the descriptions of the place are simply breathtaking.)"

Review by Indrasish Banerjee for Reedsy Discovery
https://reedsy.com/discovery/book/the-last-resort-kay-tobler-liss#review/

About the Author

Kay Tobler Liss studied literature at Bard College and Environmental Studies at Southampton College and has taught courses in both fields in New York and Maine. She worked as a writer and editor for newspapers and magazines in New York. She is the author of the novel *The Last Resort* (Plain View Press, 2020), which was nominated for a Dayton Literary Peace Prize.

Printed in the USA
CPSIA information can be obtained
at www.ICGtesting.com
JSHW071102021123
51325JS00007B/23